PHYSICALLY ALARMING MEN

PHYSICALLY ALARMING MEN

STORIES BY ERIC BLIX

Stephen F. Austin State University Press

For more information:
Stephen F. Austin State University Press
P.O. Box 13007 SFA Station
Nacogdoches, Texas 75962
sfapress@sfasu.edu
www.sfasu.edu/sfapress

Book design: Ashton Allen, Jerri Bourrous
Cover design: Jerri Bourrous
Distrubted by Texas A&M Consortium
www.tamupress.com

LIBRARY OF CONGRESS CATALOGING-IN-
PUBLICATION DATA
Eric Blix
Physically Alarming Men/Eric Blix
ISBN: 978-1-62288-171-0

CONTENTS

Bemidji / 1

Call Me Randy / 15

Golden Years / 26

Things that Drop / 44

Weatherman / 46

The Hero / 55

Rainy River / 72

Empire / 84

Doctor on a Hill / 98

Cadillac Man / 106

Physically Alarming Men / 122

Shipwreck / 133

Pool Boy / 143

To Melanie and My Family

BEMIDJI

Where else to begin but the clapboard shack? In particular, the instant in which Mr. Cotton's fist opens and the lead pipe drops to the floor, and his body topples, and he watches the blunt instrument roll across the tilted planks. Humming with an oblong whir, it comes to rest beneath the potbelly stove—empty, cold. His wide hands fasten reflexively to the knife wound in his side as he tumbles to the floor, decimated by fear and a sense of his ultimate loneliness. The brothers—these two backwoods yokels (old men who, judging by the frail sight of them, could not harm an infant, let alone a healthy man of forty)—lean against the shanty wall staring at him, hugging each other, trembling. The fat one raises his clenched hands to his mouth. The skinny one shakes and drops his knife. They are both bloody from chest to thigh. Their eyes: glossy and impenetrable, like dimes. This is the moment in which the concepts of fortune and prosperity become as distant and incomprehensible as a vellum scroll lost to a Babylonian flame, the moment in which Mr. Cotton's notion of brotherhood is cemented as something holy and inviolable. In this moment, or series of moments, which feel intelligible only in the aggregate—a spray of separate phenomena his mind fuses into a single, prolonged experience—he realizes that the coldness with which these brothers stare at him has not changed in the minutes since they saw him step out between the trees. He yelps in pain and writhes. Who will recall this moment after he bleeds out? Who will remember the silent message conveyed by these dead eyes? The ones who tell him there is no salvation to be had, not for him, at least.

Let's go back several days, to the inception of their plan, when Mr. Cotton and Sophomore and Jenny-Rosalind are huddled around the naked bulb in Sophomore's rented hotel room up in Blackduck, shades drawn. Jenny-Rosalind wears her silk nightie, though it is the middle of the afternoon. She smokes a cigarette in a bakelite holder, fanning herself with the day's paper while the men eat hamburgers with forks, because Sophomore, named for his youth and unpredictable temperament, forgot to purchase bread. Some yokel, Sophomore says, was talking about them. I overheard it at the butcher. This yokel, he's ahead of me in line chatting up some cute little blonde, and he tells her, he says to this lady, If I'm lying may the Book of Revelation come true this instant, these brothers cured me of the lump in my chest. Mr. Cotton sets down his fork, steeples his hands, and listens. Jenny-Rosalind slumps further, smiling, inhaling on the cigarette, exhaling smoke, fanning herself. I asked the butcher about it, Sophomore says, and he tells me these two brothers, they're a couple of illiterates who've got this clapboard shack, this little one-room shanty in the middle of the bog, about fifteen miles out from Bemidji. He vouched for them, too, the butcher did. He tells me his mama's parents took her out there when she was a girl, maybe fifty years ago, back when these brothers were at their peak, and they cured her baby sister of deafness. That butcher tells me that to this day his aunt can hear a fly land on a bowl of honey. How do you account for shit like that? Jenny-Rosalind throws back her head and laughs, a piercing warble from deep within her throat. Faith healers? she says. Shit, Ben, you've been reading too many of them Jesus pamphlets. Sophomore wipes his mouth with a dirty undershirt. He shakes his head. They ain't faith healers, he says. No God or Jesus is involved here, woman. The butcher, if you'd let me finish my damn story, the butcher tells me they got this affinity with the bog itself. They summon ghosts from the peat, and these ghosts enter you and cleanse your soul. The thing is that when you die, you become one of them ghosts yourself. Sophomore looks at the two of them with wide, longing eyes. Mr. Cotton feels a small tingle in his extremities. The boy's expression has a native feel to it; it's as if Mr. Cotton is peering into his own eyes, a younger version of himself staring back, expecting something. He recalls a period of life in which the thought of even a minor caper tied him into a knot of transitory, violent thrill. Past schemes appear in the space between him and Sophomore—picking the pockets of Atlantic City tourists with Jonathan, his brother (Mr. Wool); posing as icemen in pissant steel towns of western Pennsylvania and eastern Ohio, collecting dues. Sophomore forks a chunk of burger, dips it in a glass bowl of Worcestershire sauce. He chews, then swallows. He says, I heard they're part Indian. Sioux, Chippewa. Who gives a shit? You know, if we do it right, we could be millionaires.

Mr. Cotton has experience in the miraculous. A few years back, when Jonathan was still alive, the two of them and Jenny-Rosalind pilfered a milk truck and drove it all the way from Lincoln to Davenport, Iowa. Along the way, she speculated on the possible outcomes for the milkman, whom they'd pounded on the head and left bound and gagged behind a garage. He was probably fired. Hospitalized. Angry at himself, maybe at God. She'd laugh and say, No use crying over spilled milk. They bought paint in Omaha, slathered the truck in white, and stenciled in blue, WOOL AND COTTON'S CURE-ALL TOPICAL OIL: RUB MAGIC ON YOUR AFFLICTIONS AND

WITNESS MIRACLES TRANSPIRE BEFORE YOUR EYES (and beneath that, in cursive script) *testify testify testify*. Outside Davenport, they emptied all the glass jugs and metal vats into a brook. No use crying, Jenny-Rosalind sang. No use crying. Shut up with that, Jonathan said. Right god damn now. You sound like an amateur. We are not amateurs. You keep it up, and this water won't be so white anymore. You understand me? Jenny-Rosalind stayed quiet after that. So did Mr. Cotton, contemplating the sagacity of his brother's demeanor. The strong, still jaw. The wide shoulders. The unwavering stare, heavy and penetrating as a steam locomotive. Soon they reached Davenport, refilled the hundred bottles with olive oil, and parked the truck in front of Olsen's Apothecary. Jonathan stood on an upturned milk crate for four hours every day over the course of a week, barking prognostications of health and abundance to the crowd. Jenny-Rosalind would pose as a blind woman or a leper seeking help. She'd rub olive oil on her temples, or on the areas of skin she had blackened with river mud, and suddenly she'd be healed. People would gasp at the spectacle and heave toward the milk crate, waving five-dollar bills: a young boy who had been born with a fleshy claw for a right hand, accompanied by his tired mother; an old man who confessed to bouts of mania and depression, muttering about the voices in his shirt pocket; a husband and wife who showed Jonathan their handkerchiefs, stained with blood they had coughed. They all purchased their oil and left, full of hope. The pharmacy owner tried to shoo them away, first with a broom, then with a crowbar. They laughed in the man's face. The three of them pulled the same stunt all across eastern Iowa. In Donahue, Dixon, Big Rock, New Liberty. In the end, they came out ahead two hundred dollars. Enough to live on until the next grift. A basic principle under which Mr. Cotton has always operated is this: People will pay great sums to have their problems magically erased. Even if they suspect they are being cheated, the part of them that yearns for a miracle will overwhelm their sensible minds, for those who yearn will always prefer a miracle, and they will pay good money for it. This is the stuff he mulls in Blackduck as Sophomore describes the brothers. I like it, Mr. Cotton says. He pushes away his plate, offering the rest of his burger to the younger man. I think your ears have done you good today, my boy.

Morning comes. Hopes of quiet glory and brushes with the sublime. Mr. Cotton and Jenny-Rosalind head out to procure a campsite near the brothers' shack. After a half hour on the main road, they stop in Bemidji for food and supplies: beef jerky, cornmeal, sugar, a tent, pillows, blankets, gloves, boots. They take note of the hardware store and the men's shop, because, Mr. Cotton explains, they mustn't raise suspicion with a car full of dubious inventory. There aren't many purposes other than what's obvious when you put together a coil of rope and a two-foot length of lead pipe. They'll have to make several trips back to get the remainder, his suit and whatnot, his briefcase. To be discovered is to be ruined. To go about their task with calmness and deliberation, to feel the inner surge of a job precisely executed, that's the aim. Sophomore has stayed back in Blackduck, talking more information out of the butcher. (He checks out of the hotel and joins them at the camp two days later. He spends a week of daylight hours posted in the woods, observing the brothers. At night, the three of them convene at the camp, a small clearing on a bend in the creek. They burn leaves and mulch in an empty oil drum, drawing diagrams in the dirt—the shack and the landscape surrounding it; the route Mr. Cotton will take on his approach; the points in the woods where Sophomore and Jenny-Rosalind will wait, silent, sparks shooting inside them, eager to act. They speak calmly and deliberately. They commit these things to memory. Mr. Cotton stirs the fire. At the end of every night, he wipes it all away.) Mr. Cotton steers the vehicle—a hulking Chrysler—along a dirt path, which is little more than two slim ruts separated by a median of tall grass. Jenny-Rosalind smokes a cigarette out of the bakelite holder, rolling another one between her fingers. Her hair is tied into a loose bun, her features shadowed against the gray light framing her face. Mr. Cotton, working the steering wheel against the bumps and shoves of the trail, is momentarily reminded of an early job in a similar place with a girl whose name he can't recall. He was Sophomore's age, seventeen or eighteen. A little old lady lived alone in a tar paper hut beside the Missouri. He and this girl, a wild brunette, sneaked in one night on foot and stole the lady's only pair of shoes. He can't remember why they stole them. The girl's father woke when they returned, calling her name from the back room. Mr. Cotton crawled away into the trees, taking the shoes with him. They were almost caught. Jonathan smacked him on the head when he found out. He lectured on the virtues of care and craft. Mr. Cotton's vision narrows on the trail. The ruts. The grass. The canopy of trees, shading them. Something shifts inside him. The vehicle passes through alternating patches of sunlight and shadow. Jenny Rosalind sighs, snubs her cigarette, and lights the other. This job isn't like that early one. Not in the slightest.

On the shanty floor, Mr. Cotton breathes heavily. White light singes the raw edges of his wound like a conflagration. He imagines a dialogue with the hole that goes this way: Mr. Cotton says to it, Where are they? Where is my crew? The hole speaks with the overlaid voices of the yokel brothers. It says, Fill 'er up and send 'er packing. Mr. Cotton spots his hat on the floor. The potbelly stove. The windows radiating a silvery, misty light. The wool overcoat tangled around his legs. He runs his hand through his hair. Wheaty blond. There is shouting outside. Sophomore's voice. The heavy sounds of the brothers opening cabinets and moving objects. Clinking chains. Prying floorboards. Falling nails. Their whispers: like stirring stalks of grain. It's all a big gyp, the hole says. Ain't it, brother?

Years ago, when Mr. Cotton went by a different name, he and Jonathan would spend mornings helping their father gather eggs. They'd go into the coops, reach beneath the roosted hens (some would fuss and peck their hands; others would merely sleep), and they'd pull out the eggs, examining them like fine pearls. They'd place the winners in wooden crates lined with shredded newspaper. Their father would load the buggy and take it into Bismarck, ten miles away. Even at that young age, twelve or thirteen, Jonathan was an expert chicken sexer. He would gather a tiny yellow bird in his hands, hold it delicately to the light by one skinny leg between his forefinger and his thumb, and he'd be able to say with astonishing certainty whether that chick was a pullet or a cockerel, or in rare cases, a hermaphrodite. One day, after their father had left, a strange man came along on a horse-drawn cart. He parked on the road and crossed the red, dusty yard, toward the house. It was hot out. The middle of July. He wore a hat and shirt sleeves and carried a stack of Bibles, his coat draped over his arm. His cart was painted in red letters, outlined in yellow: KING JAMES BIBLES 10¢-A-PIECE. The boys were in the yard, whooping like Indians. The man set the Bibles on the porch and asked if their father was home. They stared at his pink face, wracked with chapped crevasses, an eternal squint. Jonathan picked up a chick and showed the man his skill, unsolicited. This one's a boy, he said. We call that a cockerel. He did it again, this time with a girl. The man nodded. So are your parents home, or what? he said. No, Jonathan said.

Father went to town and Mother's dead. My brother killed her when he was born. The man wiped his forehead with his sleeve. He put his hands on his hips. He was a fat man. His shirt was stained with sweat, his tie loose around his neck. Tell you what, he said, how about I leave a couple Bibles for your pa, and you let me inside to fetch, say, three quarters in return. The boys looked at each other. Jonathan set down the chick. He pointed at the lettering on the cart. That price? the man said. That's the town price. I charge a quarter in the country. He crouched on both knees, tilted back his hat, and looked around, his forehead wrinkled with scrutiny, squint widening as he spoke: You two don't want to push around a Bible man. You understand what could happen, don't you? You understand that your mama, rest her soul, could be kicked out of heaven, right? You get that? She could be kicked out of heaven and forced to burn in hell, all because you weren't willing to spare a few quarters for a Bible man. That doesn't sound fair, does it? He stood and surveyed the road. Nothing but open, empty redness. He faced the boys again. He said, How about we make a deal? You tell me the sex of another one of those chicks, and I'll let you have three for only two quarters and a dime. How's that sound? Tentatively, Jonathan picked out another chick. He wiped his nose and told the man its sex. Very good, the man said. He went inside for several minutes. The boys waited in the yard. Then he came out, took his Bibles, and left. At the camp, Mr. Cotton thinks of this incident and the subsequent beating their father delivered. It is the night before the job. They sit around the fire, huddled in the nebulous orange sphere it casts within the black night. He is wrapped in his wool coat. If he could go back, he would pound that man's head with a rock. He would summon the strength to beat that man until his fat body collapsed and his remains were slowly pecked by hens and swallowed by the dusty prairie. He would hug his brother. He would tell him it was okay, because there isn't much in this world that's worth a damn. And that's the lesson. That's the flake of gold hidden in the soot. But the others are oblivious: Sophomore runs pine spits through strips of side pork purchased with his advance; Jenny-Rosalind hums a song and smokes. They speak in hushed, careful voices about what they'll do with all the money, as if they will be happy, and the miracles they will fabricate by dint of the yokel brothers. Jenny-Rosalind will have a fancy roadster, an MG or Alfa Romeo. Sophomore, he will have a private cove someplace in the Caribbean, which he will never leave. They will convince people the brothers can exorcise demons, enhance the yields of crops, and communicate with the dead. Talk soon turns to the brothers themselves, the strange gossip Sophomore has heard. They got these oddball names, he says. That butcher told me they go three, four years at a time without contact from anyone except each other, maybe longer. They got these names they go by, because they don't remember the ones their mother gave them. The fat one is Woodchuck. The skinny one is Cup. That's how big of backwoods yokels they are. I heard them both say it, too. They sit around on that porch all day whittling hunks of peat. That's all they do. You should hear the garbled bullshit coming from their mouths. Jenny-Rosalind takes a long drag on her cigarette. She says, How's that butcher know all this if no one's been out there to find it out? Sophomore shakes his head and kicks the side of the oil drum. Sparks spray out like buckshot; the thud echoes concentrically through the woods. I been there to find it out, he says. That ain't the fucking point. Point is, these two, they wouldn't know a grift from an act of God. They're easy money, is the fucking point. They ain't even electrified yet. Shit, they pretty much eat the peat they pull from the ground. Who gives a damn what's true and what isn't? All that matters is what people think is true. What's so hard to get? Jesus, woman. Jenny-Rosalind crosses her arms. Sophomore picks up a rock, throws it into the darkness, and grins when it knocks bluntly against a tree. Later, after the three have finished a pint of grain alcohol among them, Sophomore and Jenny-Rosalind head down to the creek. Their sounds rise and swirl around Mr. Cotton, blending with the night itself. The fire cracks and hisses. He stirs it with one of the unladen spits, his soul humming with a readiness he hasn't felt since he was a younger man, persistently agitated and looking for the next perfect thing. He pulls the coat tight around his shoulders, considering how things will go: He will enlist the brothers' help, the folksy intelligence of their hands to help him rebuild the radiator on the buggy he will say broke down back there, on the road beyond the bog and trees, while he was touring the countryside with his cousins. They will say yes, or they will say no. If the former happens, the job is much simpler: A trek across the bog, into the woods. . . If it is the latter, there will be more fun. He will ask for refreshments, perhaps to wash his face, and they will oblige, as good country people do. He will follow them inside. They will talk. (The brothers do ask what's in the briefcase, Mr. Cotton eventually comes to find; they hear the sound of a blunt object sliding around, and they ask what he's got in that leather box, which is what they call it, "that leather box," much to his delight.) At some point, after they let him in, he will give the signal to Sophomore and Jenny-Rosalind—he will open a corrugated shutter and whoop like an Indian. They will come running from the woods, carrying ropes and bedsheets. There will be no bog ghosts to save these brothers. They will have crossed the threshold into their home and offered their meager conveniences to this stranger, whom they will see simply in terms of his fumbling, urbanite ignorance. Mr. Cotton stokes the fire, and he sees it all. Somewhere behind him, deep in the blackness: Grunting. Thrashing. Come on, Sophomore yells. Come on now, girl. Come get it. Jenny-Rosalind howls. God damn, Ben, she says. God damn. It is that small moment of recognition that Mr. Cotton anticipates most. That instant when the brothers figure him for a lost sophisticate, a drifting soul who means no real harm to anyone.

It is the morning of their job. Mr. Cotton rises at first light and heads to the creek to shave. After each stroke of the blade, he studies himself in a small piece of polished tin. His jaw is strong, his stare trenchant. In the tent where the others sleep, he puts on his suit and adjusts his tie. Jenny-Rosalind and Sophomore are slow to wake. He kicks the boy in the haunch. Get up, he says. Sophomore groans. My head, he says, feels like someone's playing pool inside it. Soon, they creep along in the Chrysler, approaching the wooded point of Mr. Cotton's entry. He drives slowly, tapping the brake, then the gas, then the brake again . . . In the passenger seat, Sophomore clicks his tongue, examining the length of pipe. Jenny-Rosalind smokes in back. Mr. Cotton reminds them of his rule against unnecessary killing. He says, The worst a grift can get you is a four, maybe five year bit, and that's if you're stupid and uncontrolled. His vision narrows. Dirt ruts. Waving grass. The other creatures around here are small. Chickadees. Jaybirds. Various bugs. Plus, it would defeat their purpose if the brothers wound up dead. Their purpose is key. They cannot stray. Sophomore chuckles, smacking the pipe against his palm. Relax, he says. This ain't exactly the toughest thing we've ever done. Jenny-Rosalind lights a cigarette. She crosses her legs. Mr. Cotton turns his head to Sophomore. He is frightened of what he sees: that old familiar expression, the blended textures of heedlessness and youthful abandon. The vehicle creeps forward. Mr. Cotton can hear Jonathan's mournful whisper: I'll die before I ever let a pig steer me around in shackles.

The moment of execution arrives. The car is parked back there, on the trail; his partners steal away to points beyond the shack. He can feel the cracks deepen in his persona; a light comes through: the energy that has allowed him to move from place to place with these bruising ruffians, these two hopeless fools. This light is there when he emerges from the trees. The wool overcoat is slung over his left arm, the one carrying the briefcase. He swallows. He steps forward. He waves his free arm at the brothers. The ground crunches beneath his steps. The brothers are squatted on the porch, staring at him across forty yards of open bog, then thirty, then twenty, then ten . . . The briefcase knocks against his thigh. The brothers squint. They wear linen shirts (yellowed with bodily fluids) and burlap trousers. Both have ropes tied around their waists. Bare feet. Sallow complexions. Rheumy eyes, pink and watery, glistening in the lurid glare coming through the trees. They set down their peat. They clutch their knives. The skinny one runs his thumb along the blade. Perhaps the stains are fresh, secreted especially because of Mr. Cotton. He would prefer this, that it was him who caused these recluse brothers to sweat. I don't need any miracles, he says. The cracks ramify and widen. They cast a light that only he can see. He removes his hat and holds it tentatively to his chest. The brothers look at each other, then at him. He secretes his own fluids, tears which he summons to his ducts. I just need your good graces, he yelps, falling to his knees. He wonders if this was the reason for his birth: to embed himself in the natural order of things, to reduce events to their constituent facts, and nothing else. The brothers eye each other, then him. You the tinker? asks the skinny one, Cup. Where's your wagon? Mr. Cotton tells his story. They deny him. They do not know the inner workings of automobiles, nor do they have tools beyond their hands, knives, a saw, and two hammers. He asks if he can come in, perhaps to have a drink, or to wash his face, for his walk was rugged, and he broke a deep sweat. The brothers oblige. They groan and stand and hobble in together, following their guest. The air inside is stale. Mr. Cotton sets down the briefcase. The yokels hold hands and stand against the door. Their bottom lips quiver. What've you heard? says the fat one, Woodchuck. What've you heard about us, mister? Their hands shake. Their knuckles fade to white. The skinny one pipes up, We ain't no healers. Mr. Cotton tells them to relax. He reassures them that he does not know who they are. They ask about the briefcase. He removes his coat. He begins to wash his face. And that's when things go wrong. That's when the whooping starts outside: Sophomore's reckless howls. Mr. Cotton is pitched forward above the bowl, face wet and lathered. The fat one says, You blamed cock-chafer. You devil. Cup, the skinny one, grabs his knife from the table. He holds it with both hands. The fat one slides a board across the flimsy door. They cry. Mr. Cotton lunges for his briefcase. He gets the latch unsnapped. He withdraws the pipe and turns. The skinny one plunges the knife into his side. The pain stops him upright. It spreads across his body. He looks at his red belly. The blade comes out. The blue-gray metal glints among the redness. The yokel's hand is shaky. A presence stands beside Mr. Cotton, a shadow, one he has not noticed until now, though it has been there all along. Sophomore pounds on the door. The brothers stare. It feels as if he is suspended outside time and space. The fibers that constitute each element: meaning woven of itself.

Several days earlier, Mr. Cotton purchases his suit. Jenny-Rosalind accompanies him. They sift through racks, their fingers grazing wool, until they choose the winner: a gray three-piece cut tight to his body, crisp pleats running down the front of the trousers. She flattens the lapels with her slender hands, resting them on his chest. A faint smile spreads across her lips. Look at you, she says. She grins. You ain't changed a bit since the day we all met.

The disease of homesickness corrupts his vitals: like what happens in the throes of a bitter fever, it bears down on the peripheries of his vision. He sees himself: a short, dusty child, standing in that open prairie, chickens clustered around his ankles, hair stirring in the wind. In the cabin, his body is thrown; the yokel brothers bind his hands and wrists in chains. They call each other by their strange names, Woodchuck and Cup. With their dirty feet, they kick him toward the lifted floor boards. The chickens peck the dust, searching for cornmeal, or stray oats. They glimpse the earth with stupid, vacant eyes. The brothers whimper in rheumatoidal pain. Their eyes do not shift. They stare at him with small dead apertures in gray faces. Woodchuck and Cup. He laughs. Woodchuck and Cup. The hole in his belly laughs. He tries to whoop like an Indian, but his voice won't come. A crash at the door. Pounding. Sophomore's voice. Shouting. Whooping. Instead, it's the hole that whoops. The hole sends the signal. The hole makes the sound he's been searching for. The one he only now recalls from the North Dakotan blip, long before his new name found him. Jonathan comes whipping around the house, covered in mud and feathers, whooping like an Indian. Jonathan picks up a stone and throws it at him, hitting him on the shoulder, and he whoops some more, dancing as if to bring rain. You'm be'm mine now, Jonathan says, I call'm you'm Rock Boy, and he whoops; the both of them whoop, and it seems miraculous that they can be both there and here, that they have these names. Rock Boy. Cotton. Wool. And he wonders, falling beneath the floor, hands shackled, ankles bound, lying on that dank surface of peat while the fools outside holler, he wonders how he ended up in a place like Bemijdi, so far from here.

CALL ME RANDY

(Although, I must admit, it was not entirely Mr. Redmond who was at fault. It was not he, necessarily, who caused me to "lose my cool," or who omitted any kind of meaningful intake control valve on the make and model of Bunsen burners purchased some years back by the administrators of Paul Revere Senior High School long before my sudden incarceration in March of 2007. I accept this now, that I must shoulder some responsibility for the Alleged Transgression. To "play the blame game" seems like little more than an ineffectual cop-out. There is an entire network of people, to which I am myself central, who were complicit in the so-called "senseless act of unimaginable terror.")

Of course every time I examine the nature of my house arrest, I inevitably allow for a great deal of opinion, mostly my opinion, which should not be regarded as in any way legal. Despite my superior mental firepower, I am no expert on laws prohibiting the Alleged Transgression. Which is in large part why I am here. This room is nice on most days. Mother has maintained it well. When she cleans, she addresses me by my correct name, "Randy." I close my eyes each time she dusts the bedside table and savor the word as it pours from her full lips. I observe many things. My observational prowess is quite honed. Mother's lips are first pinched at the corners and then widen into a graceful oval before finally stretching to a near-smile. This is the shape the human mouth takes when, with any of the several major American dialects, it speaks my name, "Randy." She is quite used to maintaining things—Mother was once the third runner-up Miss Montana and was therefore a minor regional celebrity in the greater Billings area for a brief period (we do not live in Montana). Just as I am now a minor regional celebrity, one much derided, although not for any of my physical anomalies (excessive beauty, which describes Mother's appearance, is a physical anomaly). I am quite tall. I towered over most people prior to my sudden incarceration early in the year 2007 (I have not shrunken yet). My shoulders are wide. I am "athletically powerful." So much so that, after Mr. Wendell "Mummy" Mumm, coach of the Paul Revere Senior High School Patriots football team, requested permission from Mother to schedule a special tryout for me, in which I participated to the fullest of my abilities, I was not allowed on the team due to my tendency of refusing to lift my knee from the windpipes of my tackled opponents. Nietzsche could very easily have said that I am the quintessential Übermensch. I have come to a new appreciation of the rigor with which Mother maintains the cleanliness of this room—the one in which I have slept since I was a tiny infant, well before my legs stretched to a full foot above the average 5 feet 10 inches height of a United States male; I would be more at home, I suspect, in the Netherlands, where the height of the average Dutch male is 6 feet ½ inch, and notions of deviance are far less genteel (I have read). My legs no longer fit my twin sized mattress. Which is to say, I am physically quite imposing. My appearance inspires extreme fear. I found this through the terrified expressions of spectators at the various public court proceedings surrounding the Alleged Transgression. It would be a mistake to call me by my incorrect name, no matter how "well-meaning" such a mistake might be.

Mother has arranged my things well. My room is quite comfortable. I attribute this level of comfort to her painstaking devotion to my happiness as her only child. This comes at the expense of her own happiness. She does not utilize her motherly talents in the other parts of our home, it seems to me. My impression is that the rest of our house has been reduced to squalor.

(Mr. Gerald Paul Redmond, an employee of the Watertown, Massachusetts local school district on a substitute basis, a mere one year after his notorious and tragic facial disfigurement, was the inaugural guest on the Fox Network reality TV show pilot, Face Lift. The show's general premise of offering charitable facial reconstruction surgery to eligible contestants who have become somehow disfigured within the last twenty-four calendar months is the obvious source of the "facial" component of its title, as well as a possible pun to the effect of the contestants being some kind of "face" for the show itself, as indicated by frequent close-ups in conjunction with long monologues by Ryan Seacrest, the host of Face Lift, describing the incredible public outreach performed by the show's many sponsors geared toward supporting the classifiably disfigured. The "lift" component is an obvious pun, as in the "uplift" produced by the contestants' individual stories of pain and suffering and televised redemption, as well as the cosmetic surgical procedure commonly associated with professional celebrities and aging women of wealth.)

Since my unexpected incarceration early in 2007, Mother has become irrevocably obsessed with the various modes of appeal granted to those alleged to have in some way transgressed the legal system of the United States of America. Her special talent in the 1977 Miss Montana pageant was multilingual oration. She now speaks "lawyerese," as well as German and English and bits of Afrikaans. Ha, ha. Each night as I dissolve particle by particle into the unconscious realm of sleep, she describes in great, beautifully structured detail the relevant legal information that could one day lead to the discovery of loopholes: that I was still a minor at the time of the Alleged Transgression; that I had suffered through years of silent bullying as a result of my gargantuan size; that media portrayals of violence left me no other option for expressing my rage.

Mother made a breakthrough early this morning. As she fluffed my pillow at my standard wake up time of 7:15 AM, she explained to me that she thinks she has a case. She has written it into her schedule to meet with my lawyer this afternoon for lunch. She will see him after she delivers my daily ice-cold 2% at noon. Which is now roughly fifteen minutes away. I always drink it from a seventy-two ounce trucker mug; the giant size reflects the extent of my thirst. The mug is embossed with a cartoon monster truck crushing much smaller sedans. I enjoy this, always. Today, Mother and my lawyer, Mr. Schatz, will discuss legal mechanisms that could potentially clear me of wrongdoing. Mother "assumes arguendo." She explained her position to me in my waking moments as she patted my pillow's soft down corners. Mother is fiercely intelligent—no doubt the source of my superior mental firepower. Sure, she said, an act of violence is an act of violence, though in my circumstance the Alleged Transgression was not done "in cold blood," nor was it unprovoked, but rather it was a response to an equally egregious and heretofore unnamed transgression against the identity of the accused (me). Namely if the accused had been properly identified by his preferred name (Randy), as opposed to his legal first name (Stephen), his own conception of himself would not have been irredeemably violated, and the "well-meaning" victim of this act of violence would have been spared, and I would not have been in the news for the duration of spring 2007, causing several school districts in and around the Boston metro area to ban the use of Bunsen burners in high school chemistry classrooms unless such use was performed by a fully licensed and certified instructor, one who was (I must assume) definitely not an incompetent substitute buffoon who could not so much as properly read a name off a class roster printed in plain English and that had been handed to him by one of the school's many administrative staff members. Hence Mother's particularly red lips and the secretion of Chanel N°5 which blooms in the space around her like great olfactory blossoms and which goes for $325.00 for a one-ounce bottle from the fragrance counter at any Macy's department store, or online. She sounds quite like Cicero, "a venerated teacher of civic virtue, the staunch republican apostle of liberty and relentless foe of tyranny" (Wood; 1998), himself the object of noble exile, whenever she decodes the various legal terminologies introduced at my bedside[1]. These dark rings, when they first developed beneath her eyes, caused her to appear battered and perpetually exhausted and possibly insane. She obscures them now with makeup. The makeup gives the appearance of dignity and rejuvenation. Her lips are artificially red. Her cheeks and forehead are blended into a consistent Anglo-Saxon flesh tone. Lunch with Mr. Schatz, who also sees to Mother's assets and I am told is a person of Russian-Jewish descent, is not uncommon in her schedule. Her makeup becomes her face each day.

Noon approaches; my daily trucker mug of 2% approaches. I have a view through a window beside my desk, which is also my workspace. This window is accompanied

---

1   I can only imagine the conversations she has with Mr. Schatz. The "lawyerese" between them must be nearly impossible to decode for those of less than superior mental firepower.

by some lovely drapes, some really terrific drapes. The drapes I could dwell on. I could describe their foundational color—a color that backgrounds the winding pattern of golden tendrils that seem to explode here and there into fat lotus blossoms (white ones with yellow stigmas, a word which confused me upon first encountering it in the botanical context I had stumbled upon online, such that I needed to google the word; I was previously much more aware of its pejorative usage, as in, "one shall be bound to exile in one's room to make phenomenological sense of the structures surrounding him, because he will have nothing else to do as he bears this deplorable stigma for having allegedly transgressed the social mores of his time"). This curtain pattern could fool one who is not accustomed to its rules. The tendrils weave and serpentine in ways that initially appear chaotic and patternless, though after heavy and persistent scrutiny, as well as a simple Google search for the manufacturer, a pattern becomes apparent, quite mechanical in its construction. The stitching is not the product of a human hand, not directly, at least, but was grafted onto this foundational color of deep and sensuous plum (or violet, or wine; no single English word exists to describe this exact color—my online searches have yielded no results, either—so I must approximate) by the cold steel needle of a heavy machine. A machine made these terrific drapes. Mother knows how to decorate both a room and her own body. She is not deceptive, though I often conflate the decorations with the things themselves—the drapes I conflate with the room, and the brilliant red lipstick I conflate with mother's lips. Just as the honorable judge Horatio Bloodsworth—who must certainly be classified as either "very overweight" or "morbidly obese" on any standard BMI index[2], given

---

[2]   I assume he suffers from the following conditions: sleep apnea, hypertension, increased risk of heart attack or stroke, type-2 diabetes, gallbladder disease w/ gallstones, osteoarthritis, gout, waking problems with respiration, such as asthma, and/or certain types of cancer (WebMD).

his miniscule height of approximately 5 feet 7 inches and his weight of about 210 pounds which I estimated as he lumbered into the Middlesex County courtroom on 23 March 2007—and the district attorney, Mr. Ryan W. Flannagan, with his requisite tie depicting the logos of all thirty-two NFL teams, each conflate the rugged strip of blackened, leathered scar tissue extending like the slick scales of a walleye pike from the "well-meaning" Mr. Redmond's dermal layer all the way down to the subcutaneous tissue on the left side of his face, with the left side of his face itself. Just as they cannot separate the Alleged Transgression from the rhetoric that surrounds it: unexplainable, horrific, YOWZAH. Bloodsworth's squatness was particularly obvious beside the fit African-American bailiff, whose head nearly reached the top of the judge's podium. 6 foot 3, 190 pounds, my estimate. I admired his rumbling voice as he read my docket number: 07-03MRSRB, which can be found on various federal and state databases.

It is especially perplexing that the good citizens of the greater Boston metro area find the Alleged Transgression so disturbing. News reports have speculated on a wave of "youth gone wild," despite my utter singularity. Perhaps on some level, members of the press are intimidated by my formidable size; these good citizens wonder how such an allegedly horrifying act of unexplainable violence could have befallen the "well-meaning" Mr. Redmond, the substitute teacher brought in to supervise the M-F 1:00-1:50pm section of Advanced Placement Chemistry at Paul Revere Senior High School on Tuesday, 12 March 2007, who wrote his name on the chalkboard in large white letters. I find the general intolerance toward the Alleged Transgression so perplexing in light of the (admittedly extra-legal) precedence set by the professional baseball player David

Ortiz, who is also commonly referred to by his nickname, Big Papi, and was referred to by his maternal surname of Arias at the time he was signed by the Seattle Mariners in 1992. Then, in 1997, he was traded to the Minnesota Twins. Upon his request, the Minnesota Twins' front office placed Arias on the official roster of their Double-A affiliate, the New Britain Rock Cats, by his paternal surname of Ortiz. This is what Mother calls an "alias," and it is legally signified by the acronym, "A.K.A.," which stands for "also known as," or in certain cases "F.K.A.," which stands for "formerly known as." Big Papi, as he is affectionately called, has so far this season smashed an astonishing 21 home runs in a mere 233 at bats and 271 official plate appearances with a slash line of .301/.393/.510 for an OPS of .903, which some years could win him the MVP award. He is indeed a fearsome presence in the batter's box, a true "over-man." And Big Papi is not the only ballplayer to come into the league with a name subject to dispute (which mine is not, as Mother knows; I am Randy). There is Roberto Hernandez, who was at one time the ace of the Cleveland Indians pitching staff under the eventually controversial pseudonym, Fausto Carmona; Satchel Paige was not actually named Satchel, he was named LeRoy Robert; there is no legal documentation that the word "Babe" should be applied as a nickname for George Herman Ruth, A.K.A. the Great Bambino, A.K.A. the Sultan of Swat, A.K.A. the Caliph of Clout, A.K.A. Jidge, A.K.A. Jack Dunn's Baby, among many other famous and generally accepted nicknames, b. 6 February 1895 d. 16 August 1948; and of course there is the commissioner of Major League Baseball, Allen Hubert Selig, who everyone knows goes by "Bud," even though "Bud" appears nowhere in his legal name. This is "only the tip of the iceberg"; baseball's professional ranks offer much in the way of precedent. Lots of physically alarming men have demanded to be called by a specific name, and their requests have been honored by the masses.

(If one is to enter the name "Gerald Paul Redmond" into the Google search bar, one is likely to find very little about the man himself. He is mainly known to the public in relation to the phrase, "senseless act of unimaginable terror," and the name, "Stephen Randall Blake." The man himself is suppressed. If one clicks on the Google "images" tab, one will see mostly photos of other men who share a name with the pertinent Gerald Paul Redmond, as well as several before-and-after facial reconstruction photos with tiny Fox Network graphics imposed on their corners. The "after" photos are similar to the "before" photos, which is likely to make a viewer feel quite sad inside, indeed.)

Of course, despite his wild popularity among "Red Sox Nation" and beyond, Big Papi is also stigmatized—his Hall of Fame credentials, even with three World Series Titles and the single season home run record for the Red Sox organization (54), are continually called into question, because he has spent his career as a designated hitter (DH). He does not help his team defensively, the argument goes. This is the stigma he bears. It blemishes his HOF-worthy statistics like a bubbled waste of scar tissue. Yet everyone calls him, like the other greats, by the name he's chosen. My stigmatization is different. No one doubts my abilities—my unmatched mental firepower and my domineering physical prowess. Ask the junior varsity running backs whose windpipes I squeezed shut with the full weight of my spectacular form, a black shadow, in their eyes, blocking out the sun.

I am in all ways restricted, despite Mother's superior aptitude for interior decoration. I can gaze at the ceiling, for instance, and meditate over the "loss of heretofore enjoyed privileges," such as the delicious and marshmallowy hot cocoa Mother would serve me prior to March 2007—I can no longer be within a 100-foot radius of any liquid, potable or not, above 100° F, according to the judge. Now she brings me 2%. It is possible for me to lie on my back many different ways, with my head at the foot of the mattress such that I must prop my enormous feet on the wall, or I can position my head more conventionally at the portion of the bed frame designated as its headboard, the posts of which are painted red while the headboard itself is painted blue, with the owner's name, in this case "Randy," my correct name, stenciled on its surface in yellow paint, resembling the haphazard scribbles of a newly literate youth. I can stare at the objects in my room. I can call this "waiting for Mother to bring me 2%." This headboard has been positioned and will remained positioned beside the nightstand holding the weak little lamp that resembles a rocket ship blasting its way into outer space. The nightstand rests directly across the room from the door, the threshold that represents the selectively permeable membrane of my confinement. Mother and the several D.O.J. representatives, such as Sheila, my leather-jacket-wearing African-American P.O.—who lacks the mental firepower to see that my stigmatization is nothing more than a breach of social protocol, and so is quite prickly in her demeanor—can come and go, while I am restricted, save for my supervised bathroom visits. I have slept in this bed since I was a spongy pink youth recently graduated from the crib to the twin sized mattress. The splendid drapes hardly seem to fit this childish milieu. I anticipate Mother's delivery of my 2% in a matter of moments. I lie on my back. My legs protrude from the twin mattress, unsupported from the knees down.

Mother announces her entry. She raps on the door frame and says her customary, "knock knock." Mother's knocks calm me. She enters and calls me Randy. She wears her finest black dress, the sleeveless one with the skirt cropped just above her knees. She sets the ritualistic trucker mug of 2% next to the rocket ship lamp. Her Chanel N°5 is pleasant and smells like her—the scent is tangled in my mind with Mother herself. It is also the scent I imagine the drapes emit when I look at them from across the room, despite their obvious scent of cotton and residual body oils from my incarcerated person. Mother, as she speaks, strokes my chest. I swallow some 2%, a large gulp. The cold milk hurts my teeth. I lean my head in a way that allows me to see the drapes on the other side of the room, and Mother assures me that I was justified in my actions, and this single act of violence does not define me, her one and only son. I ask her kindly to deconstruct her lawyerese once more. I savor her voice.

(If severe enough, scalded skin will initially turn a deep tobacco-brown. It will look immediately mucoid and infected, and it may resemble leprosy. The victim, who must be treated within twenty-four hours, will be administered many doses of resuscitating fluids, such as the isotonic solution, Ringer's Lactate, via intravenous line. A catheter must be passed into the bladder to monitor urinary output. There is a lot of gauze involved. Painkillers don't always help the way one would hope for. The affected areas must be scrubbed thoroughly with mild soap solutions. It is a miserable experience. The victim is not himself. His family may visit, if he has one. Co-workers and friends might send him flowers and balloons, and cards that read "Get Well Soon," but the victim cannot engage them. He can think only about his suffering.)

Her eye shadow is a powdery gold that sparkles when the light hits it in a certain way, and I wonder what her face would be if left undecorated, or what the window would be if not framed by the splendid drapes. Placing the empty trucker mug on the bedside table, I attempt to separate things from the ways which I conceive of them. The world as I know it filters through me. This seems like a worst-case scenario, to access the external only in terms of having been accused. It is an endless interplay of phenomena that cannot be disentangled. I curl into myself on my twin mattress and savor the aftertaste of my noontime 2%. Mother kisses me on the forehead. I hope her lips leave a red, puckered impression. She bids me goodbye and recedes into the hallway, down the stairs, I am sure, to go to lunch with Mr. Schatz. I bite the inside of my cheek until I taste blood. I wish to feel, to convince myself that regardless of any circumstance complicated by the failure of names, it—my cheek—is simply this thing we call flesh.

GOLDEN YEARS

Morris Ankney hid beneath his desk, ashamed of himself for his cowardice, hoping that if the director of business line development and implementation failed to notice him, he would be spared. Glumly, he eyed the debris on the floor—the numerous unfolded paper clips and crumpled bits of paper that had gathered in the carpet—and attached a moment to each scrap, as if the many thousands of hours he had spent working here had accumulated in small mounds of official detritus. It was a sad thought, that his years of work, which began even before the passage of NAFTA, were about to come to a swift and peculiar end. He peeked around the side of his desk. The director of business line development and implementation stood atop a pyramid of ink jet printers, snapping photos of himself with a company smart phone, reciting allusions to *Atlas Shrugged*.

"Who is John Galt?" he shouted. "I am John Galt! Everybody say it with me! I am John Galt! Oh yeah. That's the stuff!" He leaped from the printers. He licked his finger and flattened his eyebrows and snapped a picture of himself beside his whimpering secretary. So far this morning the director of business line development and implementation had fired 254 of the company's 318 employees in a hyper-efficient fever. He kept a digital tally as he went—his secretary sent out a memo each time someone was canned. He recorded videos of himself bursting into offices, kicking over cubicles, and unplugging break room appliances, telling everyone to pack it up because the party was over. He posted the videos—several dozen of them—to the company's many social media accounts, which he made entire departments watch before firing them, as well.

Morris turned his attention back to the debris beneath his desk. For every professional moment that had accumulated, there could be a corresponding number of personal ones. He and Marsha had built a house. They had tried squid ink and made a rock garden and gone to Mexico twice. They had maintained their home with prudence and diligence. Gabe—who was nearly finished with college, nearing the end of his final, tumultuous year—had grown up fast. He had turned from a meek child into an ecologically aware agitator. It was a wonder how things could change. How drastically. How swiftly.

The sound of footsteps grew. Morris peeked again. The director of business line development and implementation plodded towards him.

"Ankney!" he said, pointing a pair of scissors at Morris.

Morris's whole body filled with the sense that time had accelerated at some point long ago and launched the world far into some unrecognizable future, and he was only noticing it now, years late.

He wondered, shuffling through the increasingly empty parking lot, what he would do with himself now that he was jobless. What might his son think of him? Instead of purchasing a gallon of milk on his way home, he picked up a jug of silver rum and split it with Marsha, to whom he explained he had been let go.

They agreed to call it his early retirement. He wore his pajamas all day. He mowed the lawn in his slippers. He cooked dinner in his bathrobe and watched the news for twelve hours a day. The neighbors would see him standing on the curb, sifting through junk mail, whenever they came and went.

Marsha hugged him a lot and compiled a honey-do

list, a series of tasks for him to complete while she was at work. The first of these was to get dressed each morning, preferably something with a collar and a belt. He had time to paint the house, as well, and to re-stain the deck and finally take down the Christmas lights.

"Think of all the things you can get done," she said.

Item number two was a surprise: Stay off the internet!

He hadn't realized until he read it how much time he had been spending online in the week he'd been out of work. The videos which the director of business line development and implementation recorded had begun to crop up everywhere. Several of Morris's old high school classmates had posted them to Facebook. Digital tabloids of various political bents published them along with editorially focused tirades. People had remixed the videos, and others had made remixes of the remixes, the chant of "I am John Galt" stretched, broken, distorted, and turned on top of itself. The director of business line development and implementation's face was everywhere Morris clicked. The major business news networks all covered the rise of the mad executive, too. The narrative had somehow— inexplicably—taken flight that he made his best moves under chemically-induced fits, that it was his fury which rocketed his modest company to excessive profitability and a fast buyout from a German multinational.

One morning not long after he was axed, Morris watched a report in which the director of business line development and implementation was interviewed:

MALE ANCHOR: *Well, sir,* [laughing] *you know, I've got to ask, what do you say to average folks who might not agree with firing, what was it, three hundred people in one shot? How do you explain yourself to Main Street? I mean, it looks pretty bad to a lot of folks out there.*

FORMER DIRECTOR OF BUSINESS LINE

DEVELOPMENT AND IMPLEMENTATION: *Main Street?* [deep laughter, removes Versace sunglasses in order to dab eyes with Ceravelo ascot] *I've got one word for you, pal, and it's the most American word you'll hear all day: growth. You gotta—listen to me, hey, zoom in, cameraman. Get right in on my face. Yeah. Your producers will love this. Listen. Ready? There ain't a single thing that motivates me more, and there ain't a single god damn—*

MALE ANCHOR: *Oh, sir.* [laughs]

F.D.B.L.D&I: *There ain't a single thing more American than growth, not even Coke-a-Cola, or the stinking railroad. Growth is what I'm all about, see?*

MALE ANCHOR: *There it is, folks.* [laughing] *Attitude and all. Growth. It's the word of the day.*

The segment transitioned to commercial with a montage of photographs and video clips of the former director of business line development and implementation as he and the other directors and senior executives of the purchased company accepted both their buyout checks and their respective places on the new subsidiary's board of directors.

Morris snarled and read the paper. He cleaned out the fish tank. He scrubbed all the bowls.

By the third week of early retirement, he had whittled down the honey-do list to two easy tasks. He spent much of his remaining time sitting around the house, reading about the man who fired him, clipping articles about his old company-turned-new subsidiary, bookmarking similar websites, and researching online the possible avenues for legal action.

Could a case be made for wrongful termination?

He called one attorney, Mr. J.M. Santangelo esq., who specialized in this kind of thing. Santangelo told him the case was a lost cause.

"It's already been won in the court of public opinion," he said.

Morris sat in the kitchen and surfed the web. He made

a highball. He stroked their cat, Groucho, with his foot. He decided it might be nice to call Gabe.

"What is it?" For the last few weeks, Gabe had been in some trouble having to do with an arcane city ordinance still on the books in Ann Arbor requiring written consent from the mayor in order to harbor specific kinds of wildlife in publicly funded dwellings—even if the wildlife was in a party's possession for allegedly scientific reasons—culled from the city's charter by a very exhausted and determined dormitory R.A.

"I just wanted to chat." There was carnal snarling in the background and the sound of running water. "Is everything okay with you?"

"I can't talk right now, Pop. I'm a bit busy with this R.A. bullshit. Fighting against the malicious forces of unnatural systems, you know?"

"Right. Carry on." Morris gulped down his drink. "Be good."

He puttered around the house and drank two more highballs and read the honey-do list. He simply needed to fix a loose hinge on the vanity in the basement bathroom, which he and Marsha rarely used, and he needed to change Groucho's kitty litter, also in the basement. He figured either of these things could be done at any time, and of course Groucho's litter needed to be cleaned daily. He brought up this second point to Marsha one night, arguing that since it was in no way a major project, or even a task that required the free time and restless energy that only the prematurely retired could provide, it did not in any way qualify to be on the honey-do list. Besides, he said, Groucho was pretty much her cat.

Marsha argued that the whole point of the honey-do list itself was that she wished, in very kind, marital terms, for him to complete a given task, as in, "honey, please do this particular thing." The mere fact that she, his wife, wished he would clean Groucho's litter each day qualified the task to be on such a list. This conversation reminded her, too, they'd have to pick up Gabe from school the coming weekend, and doing so should be added to the list.

"This way you'll have the whole thing done by the time he's back."

Wasn't picking up Gabe something they would both do, he asked, and Marsha cited Groucho's litter as precedent. She smiled her motherly smile—the one she wore, he imagined, over and over again the past few decades, when Morris had worked during the day and came home at night and felt generally content in his ability to provide a pleasant and comfortable life for his family. It was the smile she wore as she'd swoop into the living room, where Gabe played with his Sega Genesis and Super Nintendo, and she'd give their son whichever baked confection she had made that morning or afternoon while reminding the boy that he could have as much as he wanted now, but he must save some for when his father would come home from work, always beat, always in need of a recipe his Urgroßmutter had brought over from Bavaria.

The next day, Morris sat at the kitchen island once again with Marsha's laptop. A picture of his old boss— grinning, mugging for the camera—loomed on the screen. It was noon or so. He swiveled the seat of the pine bar stool. He was alone.

"Guilty," he said. "That man is guilty."

Groucho weaved between the bar stool's legs. Morris clutched the grated litter scoop, which he'd carried upstairs without much thinking about it. He drank his coffee while, on the small TV beside the toaster oven, he watched his former employer force its way into the hearts and minds of the public by some perverse logic he could not begin to understand. The new global subsidiary's vice president of community interaction (the new title for the former director of business line development and implementation) answered soft-ball interview questions, backgrounded by his pool, which had a water slide, and, further in the distance so as to blur slightly, what looked like a row of tennis courts, everything surrounded by a thick cement wall latticed with ivy. This man had moved to Los Angeles, where he had apparently taken to bleaching his teeth and belly laughing. The interviewer raved about his ascot's outrageous paisley pattern.

A few days later, Morris decided to act as he supposed a retired person should.

After bagging and disposing Groucho's dirty litter, he went upstairs, through the foyer, and upstairs again to the home office/third bedroom. He opened a new spreadsheet with the idea that he would fill its cells with different items he would need to appear properly retired. He sought to choose a new hobby, which proved surprisingly difficult. He should pick something that was leisurely, slow paced while still exercising his joints, though not to the extent that his joints would be ruined, thus necessitating a different hobby later on. No model building or woodworking. No cars or motorcycles, which he knew nothing about. And he would not be henpecked like his own father, who had been a mechanic in what now felt like Morris's earlier life and spent his days drinking beer and sweeping the garage after his hands went bad. Morris wanted to immerse himself in something that he could enjoy with his son, and possibly use to tame him.

He decided to pine for the great rivers and streams of the western plains. A man in early retirement should stand for long periods in the sunlight. He should fill his lungs with clean air and restore his glow, dampened from his years spent in an office under fluorescent lights. A man in Morris's position should tie his own flies, battle the currents of brisk, clear brooks, fight with trout as he reels them in, nets them, and splits them open on the rocky shore to clean.

He filled the spreadsheet's first column with various items of fly fishing gear, neon beer signs, wood paneling, and the mini-fridge currently in Gabe's feral dorm room. He reclined in his seat with his hands folded behind his neck. He wouldn't spend his time sweeping floors in front of his disgusted son. He imagined bypassing the line of big box stores in the town's shopping district, driving down a dirt road flanked by whorls of switchgrass and bluestem. He pictured the settling dust, watched himself park his SUV in front of a slim wooden structure weathered to grayness, rendered lonesome by a flat roof and skinny windows whose sashes were painted over with white. He pictured himself in spurs. They jangled with each step across the wooden porch of this old prairie outpost. Inside he recited the items on his list one by one, and the male clerk plucked them from the shelves and boxed them up, and the two men laughed and shared several bottles of Sioux City Sarsaparilla as they compared the color and thickness of their mustaches.

There were no solitary general stores around. His most prudent options were the large strip mall on the edge of the city's retail district, or the identical strip mall in the next suburb over. He bristled when first he went to the REI for his sporting goods and then to the Home Depot attached to it for his lumber and nails, pushing the same cart at each store, which apparently was not so uncommon; no one gave him any trouble at the Home Depot for bringing merchandise in from elsewhere. He glowered at the smiling clerks.

Marsha came home earlier than usual that evening. She opened the garage door and honked, surprised to see Morris up on the stepladder with his nail gun, fastening the panels to the walls. She parked her Prius in the driveway and got out.

"Look at my manly man. What is all this?"

Morris explained his new hobby, and Marsha

approached him on the stepladder and wrapped her arms around his waist, pressing her face against his hip.

"Have you changed Groucho's litter yet?" she said.

"Of course," he said through his teeth, a quake in his gut. "It was on the list, wasn't it?"

He spent most of the next morning's drive to Ann Arbor showing Marsha how much he loved her. He used his own credit card at the gas pump. He bought her a Diet Coke. He stroked her knee and sang the lyrics of the classic rock songs on the radio. He pointed out species of birds if he knew them and made up goofy Latin names if he didn't, the Testes Maximus, the Honkus Streisandica. It was all very nice, and though he didn't have a pool or a bank of tennis courts or an artificial tan or a crazy public following, and though Marsha had asked him once again to clean Groucho's litter before they left, which he did halfheartedly, leaving the scoop in the litter box for Groucho to negotiate during his next use, Morris supposed he could live out his days this way. He had not tied any flies the previous night, nor had he done anything else that he figured would situate him in official early-retirement. The two of them watched five episodes of Law & Order: SVU after dinner, then went to bed, where Morris dreamt of violence and lawsuits.

Half an hour outside Ann Arbor, the rock station went to static, then came back as Michigan Public Radio. Some brainless montage of human interest pieces geared toward the week's market trends:

MALE GUEST: *And you know what I think is most interesting about this story, Zoe? It's that this guy—now, we all know why he's famous, we've all seen that his style of management is definitely unorthodox—the company's V.P. of community interaction, that's his title, he started from nothing. The guy grew up on a ferret farm. What else can you say, you know?*

FEMALE BROADCASTER: *A ferret farm? You're kidding.*

MALE GUEST: *That's—that's exactly where he comes from. So we know he's got this work ethic—we know—he mentions it every time he's on TV or [laughs] has he been on MPR yet?* [laughs] *Anyway—*

FEMALE BROADCASTER: [indistinguishable]

MALE GUEST: *Right? So every time he's in front of a camera or a microphone he tells us how his dad is really the one responsible for his work ethic, even if it made him a little bonkers. But hey, you know, it's why we love him, right? He grows up running around a ferret pasture changing litter boxes for, I think he's said eight to ten hours every Saturday until he figured out how to consolidate all that litter—we're talking well over a thousand ferrets, remember—into a single gigantic litter box. I guess I never even knew ferrets used a litter box* [long laughter]. *But he's the expert, not me. Some insight into his eccentric management style, no doubt, but I—I think, you know, he learned how to manage in this kind of marketplace way before it even existed.*

FEMALE BROADCASTER: *Wow. I mean, just, wow. That's so impressive.*

Marsha kept quiet. Morris gripped the steering wheel with both hands, and their SUV screamed along the interstate.

They soon pulled up in the makeshift loading zone outside Gabe's dormitory. Orange cones set off a segment of the paved outlet, where current students wearing reflective yellow vests waved orange flags to direct the flow of traffic. Students and their parents, some accompanied by young children, arranged box fans, plastic carts, and other dorm wares into the backs of mini-vans and SUVs similar to the Ankneys'. Gabe was out on the curb already, sitting on his mini fridge with several duffel bags piled at his feet. The boy was scruffy, Morris thought. His hair was pressed against one side of his head as if he'd been asleep on it for weeks, and it was long enough to become tangled with the fur lining his deerskin smock. Worse, he had a big metal cage resting on his lap containing some kind of vermin, a long skinny rodent spinning around in figure 8's.

Marsha rolled down her window. "What the hell is that thing?"

"It's the dean of student housing," Gabe said. He hopped down from the mini-fridge and met Morris behind the SUV. Morris looked at the rodent. Frizzy, scrawny, whiskers spread from a pointed snout. He asked his son what kind of animal it was, fearing that he already knew the answer, fearing that Gabe had at some point acquired an affection for ferrets. Gabe's chuckle, which was suspiciously constant, rose to laughter.

"It's a fucking American polecat. Jesus, calm down. It's, like, endangered. What's wrong with ferrets?" Gabe dropped the cage at Morris's feet, throwing up his arms at the polecat's hiss. He pranced around the side of the SUV and climbed in the back seat, where he cracked a window and slumped. Morris brought the duffel bags and the mini-fridge to the SUV in three trips. He opened the rear door to load everything, starting with the mini-fridge, which would soon be stocked with two cases of Sioux City Sarsaparilla—he could practically taste the sweet molasses already. Then he placed the caged polecat on top of the fridge. The animal had a particular odor to it, thoroughly the scent of an undomesticated body; this scent had burrowed itself in Gabe's skin. Morris did his best to efficiently fit the duffel bags in the remaining space. He pushed and labored, gritted his teeth as Gabe's voice rose at Marsha, "It grows wildly in my dorm room, okay?" The polecat snarled at Morris, as if to critique his efforts. He cringed at its fishy breath. His concentration was broken when a man, gaunt and with rings around his eyes, ran up to the SUV, straight for Gabe's face in the window.

"I hope your summer sucks shit you lousy fuck face," the guy yelled.

Gabe giggled and said, "My spaz RA. He's a slave to neoliberal power structures. Just ignore that dick."

Morris apologized to the man on behalf of his son. He considered giving him some money.

Marsha laid down some ground rules over the weekend: first, there was to be no mulch on the floor, though Gabe was perfectly free to do anything he wanted in the yard. On his first night home, he went out back after the enchilada fiesta dinner and broke a bundle of low branches off one of their oaks. He stripped the branches of their leaves and fashioned the sticks into a crude shelter. With a garden spade, he churned up a patch of dirt beneath the thatched roof and mixed in the oak leaves. This was where he slept.

"I'm lining up my consciousness with natural energies," he explained to Morris, who sipped a highball while watching the boy work.

Marsha also said there was to be no bear grease indoors (the deerskin smock was okay, however; she did not wish to limit the ways in which their son could express himself). The polecat was to remain caged and in the garage, and it was to have a separate litter box from Groucho. Groucho was not to be let near the polecat. Finally, Gabe was to help Morris complete any items on the honey-do list that Marsha added, which meant that Morris's duties did not change, and Gabe's were limited to tidying his own messes and changing the polecat's litter.

Morris had no qualms with these new rules. He didn't have much of an opinion at all. The former director of business line development and implementation was constantly on the TV—ads ran for a new reality show he was set to host about renegade executives, of which he was one. Something about firing people on-screen, Profit

Builders. Morris would browse the internet after dinner. He'd stay up late and watch the business news. He'd cut his sarsaparilla with rum and gaze out the window at his son, the animal form sleeping as man was meant to, making a life for himself in the open air amongst the creatures and foliage of the earth.

"What a bunch of reeking bullshit," Gabe said several days later, hunched and scooping. The polecat screeched, pawing at a corner of its cage.

Morris sat at his workbench watching the business news on a portable TV, sipping a glass of rum-soaked sarsaparilla. The taste bothered him. His own father had a steadfast and oft-articulated rule against mixing clear liquors with dark sodas. Morris had only completed half of the wall paneling the prior week. Today he chose to neglect the rest, tying some flies instead.

"You learn to deal with it," he said.

Gabe stopped scooping, looked over his shoulder at Morris's back. "This is what you do all day, then? Scoop cat shit and fuck around in the garage? I'd kill myself."

"For crying out loud, Gabe. Stop criticizing. Just do what your mom wants."

"What? I'm already over this shit. I've got big plans."

"Oh yeah? And what are those?"

Gabe spun the plastic grocery bag he'd scooped the litter into and tied its handles. He grabbed a handful of kibble from the shelf by the door and dropped it in the polecat's cage. The thing was ravenous, squeaking and grunting as it ate.

"I don't know yet. Something crazy. Like that ass wipe that fired you."

Morris set down his pliers. He cautioned Gabe that the man who forced him into early-retirement—this life of scooping Groucho's waste—was not to be mentioned in this house. Gabe brought up the inconvenient fact that

Morris had not watched anything except the business news networks since they'd been back from Ann Arbor, that the business section of the daily paper was always spread open on the kitchen island—the guy's face was everywhere in their house.

"If you hate him so much why don't you get revenge? I fucking would. It's part of a natural system of completion." He patted the polecat's cage. "It's better than stroking your dick in this stupid garage all day."

Morris kept quiet. His own father had rarely spoken, and suddenly he felt like he was back in the garage of his childhood home, dropping screws into a used coffee can, little metallic clinks matching the rhythm of his father's broom strokes, as if to mark the passage of time.

He shrugged, sipped his drink.

"Fight or flight," Gabe said. "It's pretty basic shit."

Later in the day Morris went online. He scrolled through different flies that he feared were already lacking from his tackle box. He sipped from a fresh bottle of Sioux City Sarsaparilla cut with silver rum, wiped a slight film of boozy drink from his mustache. Downstairs, Gabe yelled something at the polecat, or possibly at Groucho. Morris gazed at the boy's bed of leaves through the window. He examined the floral print of the home office/third bedroom's wallpaper.

The air in this new phase of life felt depressingly stale, like he was nothing but a giant mote of dust. Before purchasing the flies, he decided to check out ticket prices to Los Angeles. He was surprised, even happy, to see that he could fly out the next morning for only $300.00 per adult passenger, round trip. He refrained from taking another sip of his makeshift cocktail. He booked two tickets. He leaned back in his seat, crossed his arms, and put his feet up on the desk. He called Gabe upstairs and asked him if he'd like to go out west.

"What, with you?"

"Of course," Morris said. He explained that it was a kind of business trip.

Gabe smiled and crossed his suntanned arms. He said, "So long as you don't walk around taking pictures like a dipshit tourist. And we better not end up on the beach. I fucking hate sand."

Marsha was glad to hear that they were going on an overnight fishing expedition together, just a father and his son, though she feigned distress: how could she binge on gouda and wine if she had no one to clean the two litter boxes in the house?

At the airport, the TSA agent pulled two sharpened sticks from Gabe's burlap duffel bag.

"What are these?" he said. Morris watched the guy examine them; the agent turned and felt their pointed tips, scrunching his brow into a strained cleft. Morris clutched his own briefcase to his chest—filled with résumés and maps of Californian trout streams he'd printed off and shown to Marsha. He glared at his son.

"Pop's taking me out to L.A. to become a big time drummer," Gabe explained. "I'm a naturalist. The sticks are my schtick." He drummed his belly with open palms, bobbing his head to the beat.

They landed at LAX at 11:00am, PST, claimed their luggage, and wheeled it outside to catch the shuttle to the car rental kiosk. The heat and smog sizzled on their skin and jammed up their wind pipes. At least, Morris assumed it was smog that choked him, although Gabe, the philosophical ecologist-in-training, insisted that it was airplane exhaust.

"Hey," Gabe added, "what's Mom gonna do when she looks at the credit card statement and sees we didn't go fishing? You gonna get divorced? Have yourself little mid-life ordeal? Find a nice studio downtown and meet your muse late in life?"

"Can it."

"Boy oh boy, Dad's out for blood. This V.P. of whatever better watch his squishy pink ass."

The shuttle soon arrived. As it made its way to the car rental kiosk, the driver asked where they were off to. Morris told the guy they were going to Bel Air to meet up with an old business associate. The guy called Gabe "Tarzan" and joked that they should be taking a limo, but when neither Ankney laughed he warned them about the traffic around the airport. The 105, he said, was not so bad, but once you turned onto the 405, watch out, it'll be like you've been marooned. He examined Gabe head to toe in the rear view mirror.

"Have you been marooned?" he said.

Morris and Gabe nosed onto the 105 in a Prius not unlike Marsha's, though it was two years older and had logged 80,000 more miles than her's. The traffic was steady enough for Gabe to make metaphors: it was the natural course of a human life full of difficulty and compromise; it was the unavoidable division between us all; it was the slow and steady flow of time itself. As they approached the 405, however, Gabe decided that traffic was the clogged artery of the industrialized world. All six lanes were backed up, cars from each squeezing toward the single-lane on-ramp.

"Look at us," Gabe said. "Two clumps of litter stuck in the same smelly box."

Morris ignored him. He turned on the car's radio and scanned the stations until he found a traffic report. The outlook was bad. It seemed as though they'd run into a particularly heavy traffic jam, one that had the radio announcer questioning his ancestors' decision to go west to the Pacific. Morris surveyed the vehicles ahead, then those in the rear view mirror. Nothing but gridlock. Then he stared himself in the face. Stubborn. Idiotic. Like his own father, insisting that it wasn't so bad to live a life drinking and doing chores. What would he even do if he actually made it to the the director of business line development and implementation's mansion, past the cement wall and security gate and, he imagined, the pack of rabid ferrets that protected the estate's front lawn? He looked at Gabe, who pulled a handful of edible roots from his smock and munched. The boy waxed philosophical, noting that at this point, nothing that Morris did would matter, because the system he was fighting was not a natural system and had no internal logical-biological apparatus to introduce alternative ways of being.

"It doesn't really make any sense. It's pretty fucked up."

Tail lights and hazy morning air. Drivers, including Morris, honked and cursed at each other. Morris clutched the wheel. He thought of the collective minutes being spent by people stuck in various automobiles, time turning to vapor like hot exhaust. How many hours, or years, or decades were lost to the air per second? He recalled a memory of his childhood garage, a moment he hadn't thought of in years. He had opened the door from the kitchen to call his father for dinner, and saw the old man on his knees in the darkness bent over a shattered bottle, blubbering and sucking suds off the swept floor, and Morris, only a boy, had felt as if he then knew what it meant to be ruined. He turned to Gabe and wiped away a tear, cursing the forces of the universe. He rolled down the window and stuck out his head. "Move it, you silicone bastards! My son and I have business to take care of!" He revved the Prius's pathetic engine and vowed to continue onward toward Bel Air.

THINGS THAT DROP

My mother used to say, "Just make sure your bills are paid on time," which I explicitly remember her saying once when I was seven and wanted to talk with my grandmother (who lived in Florida) on the phone, and our phone was disabled for reasons that were mysterious to me then but fully comprehensible to me now. The saying, "Just make sure your bills are paid on time," has the cadence and solemn humor to be something of a mantra, or a slogan, or a personal motto. I imagine she said it many times about various things (the water, the heat, the credit cards).

Something upstairs drops to the floor and rolls across it, which if the floor of the upstairs apartment is anything like mine—this seems likely, that it is similar or identical to my apartment—then it is a sickly green enamel laminate with decorative color blots—red, yellow, white—dotting its surface seemingly without method or control. The color blots are scattered as if blown from an upturned palm.

This thing that has dropped from some surface sounds like a marble, or a BB, or a ball bearing. I imagine it fell from a table. This happens several times each day, though not at the same time each day, but at arbitrary times. Noon, for example, or much later. Sometimes I am in bed, sprung to sitting when I hear this object fall and roll, gaining an increasing awareness of where I am and what has startled me. In these times, when the fallen and rolling object wakes me, or disturbs my efforts to sleep and so shifts my focus from my inability to sleep to the skittering above me—the initial tap and the subsequent sound of rolling away—the orange cat leaps to my bed and brushes against me, asking in his way for me to fill his bowl. I get up at these times and do not fill his bowl but instead refresh my browsing window, so that the streamed episode of *SVU* or *X-Files* is no longer timed out, and I can refocus on sedating myself with the sounds of police procedure, courtroom drama, and alien investigations.

At other times I am at my desk, doing whatever. Work. Surfing the internet.

Now, I intend to call home. I intend to catch up with my mother and father and learn of my siblings' updates. My phone has no service.

Two men direct each other outside; they are moving a sofa into the apartment below mine.

"Turn it," the one says.

"I can't," says the second. His voice is much gruffer than the other man's. "The door's in the way."

"Back it up. Back it up."

The thing upstairs drops, the BB or ball bearing, or the marble.

I am habituated to the existence of this sound. I close my web browser. I wait for the object to tap again, and in the meantime wonder what goes on up there between taps, if they, the man and the woman who live there, are playing with marbles as I and my several cousins used to when we visited my grandmother's house, or if they are loading their own shot gun shells to massacre the other tenants with, or if they sit on opposite sides of their table, wondering what they should each say next, and the man plays idly with one of the many small sapphire zirconias they keep in a decorative bowl at the center of the table, and it falls from his fingers, rolling underneath the refrigerator where all the others have gathered.

WEATHERMAN

In the waiting room, the nurse calls my name. I pocket my phone and take notice of a little girl sitting across the way from me. She stands upright in the seat next to her mother's, leaning her shoulders against the wall and grinding her heels into the chair's fuzzy blue upholstery. Her arms are wrapped around her body—she appears to be hugging herself, though I can hear her angry breaths. An older man sits at a right angle to me on a bench-style seat. This man asks the nurse to repeat herself, apparently thinking he may have been called. His wife tells him it's not his turn, it wasn't his name. She explains this slowly.

It's a strange mix outside, small patches of sunlight, pellets of sleet that tap against the waiting room's skinny windows and melt when they hit the ground. The seats in here look somewhat comfortable, but they are actually incredibly stiff and poor to sit on. I grunt as I stand. I nod to the elderly couple, but I'm not sure they notice. My knees both pop. The nurse is extremely young. My instinct is to doubt her qualifications. The long ponytail tied at the exact top of her head with a banana-yellow band, the strawberry perfume, the pink lip gloss; I can't imagine her sitting in a classroom, learning how to measure blood pressure or administer shots or work the ultrasound equipment. She should be at the mall, I think, looking for fashionable items at the cheapest possible prices, mini skirts and shoes, or she should be on the arm of an older man (old enough to be her father, at least), a steely management type who shows her off at company functions and spoils her at home—this is Uncle Ron coming through me, I realize. I tell him to shut up. Silently I beg.

I catch the little girl's gaze as I go past, and notice that a mottled red rash envelops her left arm. She tries her best not to scratch it—I can see in her face, her welling eyes, especially, that the rash itches unbearably. The little girl's mother reads a People Magazine. She licks her thumb and turns the page. This nurse is perfectly qualified, I'm sure. She's probably given a million echocardiograms to a million different guys with hearts in much worse shape than mine.

I am my mother's only son. Ron was the "male influence" in my life after Dad passed away a week before my high school graduation. Six years later, after Ron went, I was the male influence in my own life, and I have been ever since. Brothers, they both went by way of massive coronaries. It is a burden carried by the men in our family, that we are predisposed to catastrophic heart failure. The importance of annual physicals has been central to my adult life. I visit Mom three evenings each week at her assisted living facility. This has been the routine for several years. She reminds me of my physical each fall in the same way she reminds me to wear a coat, as if I simply don't know to do it.

"Your dad might still be alive if he ever went to the doctor," she says, and she still gets weepy.

In November of 1981, two weeks before I turned 16, it was the five of us on Family Feud. Mom, Dad, me, Ron, and a second-cousin, Grace, posed in an old-timey tableau behind the giant placard depicting our family name (Grace's last name was different, though I don't remember what it was, exactly; this was part of the vast artifice of Family Feud). Mom sat on Dad's lap with her legs crossed. Dad kept one hand on his knee, the other on the small of Mom's back. His back was rigid. From where Ron and I each stood (a hand on the others shoulder and our free arms crooked at the elbows in some folksy hee-haw fashion), I could see the long lines around Dad's mouth. The fact that people called them laugh lines seemed strange. And Grace stood with one leg propped on an upturned soap box with her blue skirt lifted and ruffled above the knee. Ron noticed this.

"Hey," he whispered. He flicked his eyes toward Grace. "How about that second-cousin?"

Now, the nurse records my body weight. 180 pounds, not bad for my age and height, but it's a little high. She asks me if I exercise. I'm not sure whether to interpret this as a medical question or a personal one. I tell her that I run when I can. She grins and asks me how often that is, specifically. I could kiss her.

"Maybe once a week, sometimes," I say, and clear my throat. She nods and tells me to follow her. We head to the examination room together. I stare at my feet as we walk.

Sometimes I wonder about dementia. I ask myself which would be the better way to go: suddenly while still young, a final jolt through the chest, or to slowly dissipate, already deep into one's old age, spread a little thinner each day like the thunder claps of a calming front, until there is silence, and life is altogether gone. What would 100 randomly surveyed individuals choose? I imagine the first scenario happening at a candlelit dinner table with a date not unlike this nurse. There are flowers pinned to our clothes, a rosy glow in her cheeks before my heart explodes in my chest. A glass of wine spills as I grasp at the white table cloth and rip it with me to the floor. People around us gasp. Occasionally someone pleads for a doctor in the house. In the second scenario, I see myself on my back attached by plastic tubes to different beeping medical devices. In this scenario, I am the same off-yellow as my bedsheets, which are soaked with the oils secreted by my failing body, as though I'm melting slowly into my death. I am recalling unrelated memories, deliriously reliving them—the time Ron stole six dollars from Mom's purse to buy a carton of cigarettes: "I'm cool, I won't tell anyone," I say; Dad, with his typical deliberation, sanding the flat surface of the garden bench he made for Mother's Day when I was nine, and I ask him, "Can I try, Dad? Dad, can I try?" I speak into the empty room as I grow more and more invisible. To whom do I recall? No one. There is no one left. Dad was in his early sixties and getting by okay; only his knees ever bothered him. Ron was 45 and in otherwise perfect health. He was discovered in his garage by a neighbor, a can of motor oil tipped over on the workbench and his Bronco's fluids pooled around him on the cement floor.

When the Family Feud PA announcer called our name, a couple of crew members drew the placard to the side with ropes and pulleys, and we all sprung down to the long yellow podium on the floor of the set. The crowd was not the horde I'd imagined going in—maybe forty people clapped and hollered when Richard Dawson sashayed onto the set. Mom wore a red boutonniere on her brown dress, expecting it to match the host's. Richard Dawson's, however, was a floppy white petunia. He made a joke out of the discrepancy and called her darling. The crowd's laugh was underwhelming. Richard Dawson kissed Mom on the lips and Grace on the back of her hand. Mom was starstruck for the rest of the taping, offering absurd guesses to every survey question. When Richard Dawson asked for something you put on ice, Mom said more ice. Dad stood tall and gave terse answers. One word here and there, "trumpet," "groceries." He was apparently a very funny man in his younger years. He had the kind of humor that allowed others to go silly with laughter while he remained his stoic self. I have early childhood memories of accompanying him to the hardware store. In each of these—which are possibly not even separate memories, but a single instance mutated into many forms by hindsight—he'd drop a sack of nails on the counter and speak of crucifying himself. The clerk's face would wrinkle in laughter, and Dad would say something like, "I live life nail by nail." I never witnessed his humor the same way others did. I never found him witty. Ron did, though. We smoked cigarettes in the alley behind the church on the day of Dad's funeral.

"That son of a bitch," Ron said. "This is probably just some big punchline to him." He had on the only suit he owned—a hand-me-down from Dad, blue, too wide for Ron's bony frame. The only other time I ever saw him wear it was his own funeral.

Now, the sweetheart nurse asks me what I do for a living. She drops my file in a plastic slot mounted outside the examination room door. I tell her, and she says, "Very interesting."

"You bet it is," I say. I hand her my coat. I know a thing or two about self-crucifixion: we make brief eye contact; she clears her throat and asks me to sit down on that little stool right there, the spinny one, because she needs to ask me some questions about my medical history before we can move on with this procedure.

Back in 1981, in the triple money round, I choked. Richard Dawson leaned in, and I could smell his musk and, from the folds of his suit, the smoky residue of unjustifiably cheap cigarillos. He asked me for something that fathers teach their sons.

"Doing your taxes," I said, and the crowd groaned, suddenly very loud. Dad glared down at me. I tried to imagine him holding a rubber chicken by its neck. Grace, whom I've never seen since the Family Feud taping, fell backward. Her skirt lifted to reveal her thighs. Richard Dawson stared at her with his eyebrows raised, then he turned to Ron and me, smirking. He quickly composed himself, covering the microphone on his fat lapel with his blue note cards and clearing his throat. He told me that it's okay, they can edit it out and give me a second chance if the other family—the Kerns, the four-time returning champions who were on their second taping of the day— approved. They didn't, of course; they wanted to pummel us. Ron laughed his ass off at my answer. He grabbed my shoulder and repeated it toward Richard Dawson, who'd already committed to the commercial break, strolling off the set and lighting up with the sound crew, looking over his shoulder at Grace every now and then after she sat up, dazed; his petunia wilted in the smoky huddle. Though we didn't win any money, they sent each of us home with a film strip of the episode. Any time we wanted to, we could watch the Kerns, who all had the same gap-toothed grin, nail the fast money round. I've never been sure how their family decided to divide the prize money. Dad would have placed it in a family trust if we had won. I would have been angry, because I'd have wanted something fun, a VCR or a Trans Am, even if I had to get one that was a little used, but deep down I would have known him to be right. I've since had my copy digitized. I watch it sometimes if I've had a couple of drinks, or if the traffic outside my apartment is light and the sounds of life don't filter in so well, or if I have any kind of medical procedure the next morning, however minor. I study my hair in the video, the center-part and the feathered bangs. I see Ron's grin and remember how it looked with a cigarette punched through it. My parents are well behaved for the cameras. Grace giggles almost constantly. We look like a TV family, I think. I always imagine Dad sitting on the couch beside me, looking over his folded newspaper. He studies Mom and jokes, "If I didn't know better, I'd think she was your mother," then he returns to reading about his NASDAQ investments. I never crack a smile.

Mom's lips were inflamed for two whole weeks after

kissing Richard Dawson. While she was doing the dishes, licking the balm off her puffy mouth, Ron took me into the garage and gave me my first beer ever. He eyed me up and down, stopping on my knobby elbows and my worn out Black Sabbath T-shirt.

"Anyone tell you yet how to fuck a girl?" he said. I blushed and told him no. He sipped his beer and explained the nuances of attracting a 17 year old sex partner. I tried out some of his suggestions. I slapped Mandy Davis on the ass at school and grinned at her, but I was sure my face was all wrong. I said there was more of that under the bleachers. Of course it didn't work.

"Hey," Ron said, "no one bats a thousand." He blotted his cigarette in the ashtray next to Dad's easy chair (another bit of evidence for my Dad's odd humor: he wasn't a smoker; the ashtrays were for soaking his cuticles). He changed the subject to the difference between single and triple malt scotch, opened the liquor cabinet, and saw the only whiskey we had was Wild Turkey. He shrugged and pulled from the bottle, then held it out for me to take a drink. He said, "How about we go laugh at them lips on your Mom? I think Dawson gave her herpes."

Now, the nurse asks me to remove my shirt. She asks me how work is going, and I tell her it's stressful as always. She asks about my tobacco and alcohol consumption. I'm a non-smoker and a social drinker, I say. Then she asks me if I've ever had an echocardiogram before. Her scrubs are pink with little blue balloons. The seams run in close to her body at the waist. I'm certain that she hates the chunky white sneakers she has to wear.

"Every year," I say. I preemptively tell her about my family history. My dad, when he went, was much older than I am now. Ron was two years younger.

She enters my information into a computer at the little desk in the corner, making chitchat as she turns off the light and wheels the ultrasound machine to the examination bed.

"Strange weather," she says. Her pony tail bonces lightly as she moves. "Seems like it's 50 degrees outside one day, then the next we get snow."

I agree with her while I wonder if I could get by in life kissing every woman I meet on the lips. She explains the procedure out of what I assume to be her legal obligation. She'll be taking pictures of my heart, essentially, to make sure it's functioning the way it should. Every measurement she takes is standard. She is not allowed to tell me if they do or do not appear normal. She talks to me like I'm a child. I don't mind this; I do as she says. I lie on my side and breathe slowly while she boots up the machine. I watch her apply the blue gel to the sensor, which resembles an electric razor, though it's larger and white and has a cord running out of it. She hums to herself, and I try to recognize the song. It occurs to me that Ron's influence is coming through me again. It's one of his old tricks. When I couldn't get Mandy Davis behind the football field, or when my second-cousin Grace asked me if I had tried to glimpse her panties when she fainted on the Family Feud set—when I was caught in my bedroom practicing with the clasp on an old Playtex of Mom's I'd fastened around my pillow—Ron instructed me how to play possum. Act injured, gain sympathy, get fucked. A sprained ankle playing basketball, a bust-open lip defending a weak classmate from a bully. The nobler the better.

"Possum is pussy," he told me, and, in this darkened examination room now lit only by the ultrasonic screen, I swear I can hear him say it to me again.

"Possum is pussy." There it is.

The nurse, who I remind myself is perfectly qualified, touches the sensor to my chest. The gel is cold. She shifts as I do. When I swallow, so does she. Her motions mimic mine.

Suddenly I can see my own heart. It happens every year, but it's always a surprise. Black and white and kind of hazy. I can hear my pulse throbbing behind my ears. I watch my heart valves open and close. It's like being up close to a snorting bull, this thought that it's *my* heart I'm looking at. Soon streaks of color appear on the screen. A red portion turns to blue, a strip of green cuts across my heart like a tiny storm front. The nurse pushes buttons. She captures images of my heart as it's broadcast to me, my life force depicted on-screen.

"Possum is pussy," I can hear it again.

This nurse has a father, living or dead. It's likely that he's around my age, whoever he is, however involved he is in her life. I like to imagine that he's exactly twice as old as she is, that he's proud of her and offered to put up half of her nursing school tuition money even though he couldn't technically afford it, and that he brags to everyone he knows—the guys at the garage, his companions at AA, to whom, he says, she is his Higher Power—now that his daughter is a real live nurse. My baby helps people, he tells them. She scans their chests with her special equipment, and she can see inside. It looks like weather patterns, it truly does. Like little Doppler radars. And my little girl does this for a living. She could do it to you or me if we needed her to. You could come to her with a pain in your chest, or even a tiny little flutter, and she could turn on that machine of hers. She understands what she sees. She might know you more than you know yourself. She can be your personal weatherman, and together you can watch the storms that rage inside.

THE HERO

The hero arrived with his convoy, and suddenly the bowling alley wasn't so quiet. Jolene watched them pass through the arcade, twisting between the sticky round tables people rented for children's birthday parties. She rested her elbows on the counter. Her belly pressed delicately against the cash register. It was really him.

Two figures led the procession. Their suits were black and cut tight to their bodies, which seem cast from graphite molds: identical GI Joe dolls fresh off the assembly line. They crouched low and spoke into their shoulders and checked under tables and around corners for possible danger. They signaled to each other with their hands, as if a terrorist might lurk in a bowling alley. A gaggle of photographers and cameramen crowded around the hero. A director—short and fat and red-faced—barked out commands: "You're missing your spot, Reginald!" shoving a photographer in the back, into position; "I need more light! Where is all the light? Has God forsaken this place?"; "Smile big, Mr. Hero! You're in close-up!"

One of the hippies on lane ten rolled a gutter ball and gawked stupidly at the commotion. Jolene had been spraying a pair of shoes, which somehow ended up in the trash can.

The hero waved at the hippies and joined their game. He rolled three consecutive strikes with a 35-pound house ball. Like most folks, he bowled right handed. The director took off his purple beret and waved it around, positioning cameramen here and there. He commanded the hero to set up a 7-10 split, which was successful after several takes. Then, as per directions, the hero covered his eyes with his right hand and rolled with his left. The ball coasted down the center of the lane, between the pins. The cameramen only captured his release. They took pictures of him smiling.

"Very good," the director said. "A little stock footage, Mr. Hero, and the pro circuit might come calling for your services."

Marco scurried out of the back room. He had a clipboard and a half-full ice bucket.

"What's this noise?"

"That hero that's been on the news lately just came in," Jolene said. "Him and a bunch of other dudes. I don't know, his crew or something."

The director clapped his hands and stomped laps around the ball return station. "No no no no no!" he bellowed.

"Jolene?" Marco said. "What the hell are you doing?" He set his clipboard on the counter and handed the shoe spray to her. "Is your water broken? Get these men some shoes."

The hero posed for pictures with the hippies. He was handsome. Stunning. Perfect. His smile was symmetrical, possibly enhanced by surgery; his teeth were whiter and more square than any Jolene had ever seen, at least in this town. Little baby feet kicked the inside of her belly, which was the size of the bags the league players all owned. What would her life be like if Carl had been a hero instead of a mongrel redneck, the kind that married a woman, impregnated her younger and impressionable sister, then ran off to North Dakota when he heard his cousin was making nearly one-hundred-thousand dollars per year twisting bolts on oil rigs?

"I could twist a dang bolt," he'd said.

She sneered. Fat pig.

"What?" Marco said. He was staring at her, pitched

forward with his hands held out, belly hanging over his belt like a tarp full of rain. He'd missed the spots of shaving cream behind his earlobes that morning. "You don't know how important the hero is? That man could be our next president. Don't you know that?"

"I know just fine." She shuffled over to the beer pumps and shouted into the bustle to ask if anybody wanted a pitcher. The hero was busy rolling more strikes. The crew documented him. Camera flashes. Boom mics. The hippies stared. The director fretted and pulsed, like a flower continuously switching from wilt to bloom. Jolene filled two pitchers: one for the convoy, one for herself.

"To good men everywhere," she said.

The director threw down his fists and twirled away from the camera crew, who were apparently slacking, or misunderstanding his directions, or making artistic choices of their own. Jolene caught his stare. He gasped, clutching his chin with both hands, and tears welled in his eyes.

"You poor creature!" He sailed to the counter in several strides and stroked her face. "Disaster has befallen you. I can sense it. Your eyes are troubled and your skin is ash." He took the beer cup away from her and called over a cameraman. "How old are you?" he asked, sliding his card across the counter: Roman A. Clef, Director & Auteur.

"How old am I?" Jolene said. She stuck the card in her pocket.

"Yes. Your age. What is your age? How much time have you spent on the planet Earth?"

"I'm twenty-one and a half."

"Oh." He sucked his lip and pressed a hand contemplatively against his cheek. "Twenty-one and half? No. That can't be right. I would have guessed forty or forty-five. Twenty-one and a half? You're sure?"

"Sure as that stupid hat on your head, Mr. Clef." She took the cup back from him. His torso was short and round and silly-looking beneath the lacy pleats of his shirt.

"It's pronounced clay, you primitive dingbat! As in, that grout stuck beneath your fingernails! I'm afraid you simply won't work for us. See, if you were forty-five, or even forty, then I could depict you as a miracle. You would *be* a miracle. A forty-five year old pregnant woman, touched by the hero. See the angle?" The director sniveled and called off the cameraman, who hadn't come anyway, but sat at the scoring table instead. Jolene swigged the remainder of her beer and told Marco, who sneered at her, disgusted, that she was going on break.

She'd first decided the hero was a sexy MF when she saw his face on all the magazines at the supermarket. She'd gone there quite a bit lately to assuage her cravings. At first she only wanted to eat tuna fish straight from the can, then after the first trimester, she started eating it with Hungry Man dinners. One night, as she sank back into the sofa watching Jeopardy, she dwelled on the remains of food on the coffee table. A plastic tray she'd microwaved too long, singed on the edges. White flakes of canned fish mixed with gravy, stinking up the inside of her trailer, planting itself in the upholstery of her sofa and her velvet prints of Christ. After that night, she'd started strolling through the fancy food aisle and buying chicken pâté instead. She spread it on top of the Hungry Mans. Everything was microwaveable, which was good, because she'd never learned anything about ovens or stoves from her mother, who was also named Jolene, just different ways to open a twist cap—on the counter top, between her titties, depending on the situation.

She went outside for a smoke while the hero and his crew bowled. Her thing was to lurk around the dumpsters on the side of the building. She never told Marco about the cigarettes, because he took it upon himself as daytime manager of Family Time Bowl N' Play to shame her for drinking and smoking with a baby in her belly, and she didn't like that. She couldn't take that shit coming from him, like he was some health nut with a wall of diplomas and certificates he could point to as proof of his superiority. He probably hadn't seen his dick since he was in Sunday school, maybe even a crib. He might not know what his own appendage even looked like. Instead, she'd always tell him she felt faint and needed to walk outside.

The parking lot opened up to the highway, across which was the snowmobile plant, a long structure of prefab concrete and corrugated sheet metal. She could hear the shrill wail of Snow Cat engines in the test field behind it. It always seemed stupid that they fixed wheels to the skis and tested these things in the summertime, when no one except the testers or redneck idiots like Carl would drive their sleds. Dummies. A whole town of dummies and rednecks.

She took a long drag. More kicks in her belly.

The hippies came sashaying out of the entrance grinning and piled into a brown Dodge. The one driving slumped in his seat and drove slow, as if he was an old lady on her way to the beauty shop to get her dye job touched up. Dummies.

The hero had come in a black SUV, like what the president would ride in. Had he ever flown in a helicopter? That was something Jolene would like to try. She saw a movie one time where they flew a helicopter down low and pulled a drowning man from the ocean. They dropped a flotation device to him on a cord, and when he grabbed it, they raised the helicopter and flew off with him dangling there, a good thirty feet below the cab. She pictured herself wearing goggles and a pilot's helmet with one of those little microphones on it like the pop stars wore on stage. Between her legs, dropping out the side door that never seemed closed on a helicopter, hung her umbilical cord with her baby at the end, sleeping above the lapping white waves with her thumb in her mouth, peaceful as a bee on a bed of pollen.

She hated picturing what the baby might look like after

it was born. In her mind, it always came out pregnant, a baby-within-a-baby, as if Carl's seed was powerful and angry enough to knock up consecutive generations. She snubbed her cigarette on the side of the bowling alley, taking a second to admire the new spot of char, a small black circle beside the old ones she had left on previous smoke breaks. The little girl would be named after the family tradition of misery—little Jolene the Third.

The SUV, a Cadillac Escalade, was clean and waxed and sparkled in the sun. A sexy vehicle. It might be just as exciting to ride in one of these as it would be to fly in a helicopter with her daughter dangling from her, still attached to her uterus. She looked down at her feet in her dirty white flip-flops, then at the T-shirt Carl had given her: a souvenir from the Kid Rock concert in Grand Forks several years ago when he was still her brother-in-law. Her blue sleeves, her white torso, Kid Rock's ugly chin stretched wide around her stomach. Whoever drove the Escalade had forgotten to lock it. She opened the door and felt the seat. The leather was unlike anything she had ever touched in her life. It was truly soft, not like her sweatpants, which had been washed so many times that the cotton felt like another layer of dry skin. Maybe it was fetus leather in this SUV, a substance so immaculate and pure that the only way to explain it was that it had never roamed the earth. Or the hero's ass had transmuted it into a divine substance, skin peeled from the Lamb of God.

The Snow Cat engines wailed and cluttered the sky. Jolene hardly noticed them. She was thinking about how her baby might be affected if she got in the SUV. A cleansing before birth, or a blessing, a kiss on its little forehead from the almighty lips of God.

She had to sit on that leather. She just had to.

After a while, the twin guards found her in there curled up with her thumb in her mouth. She had drooled on the seat.

"You have to get out, ma'am," the one said.

"This is no place for a civilian," said the other.

"I'm sorry."

"You have to get out."

She lifted her head. Had she been sleeping? Visions of Carl out in the oil fields, slicked with crude like he was something awful emerging from the earth. Fires blasting over his shoulders, the smell of brimstone and the pained shouts of oilmen percolating the red wastes. She thought the desert was supposed to push up bleached bones. Mule skulls and the crawling limbs of the terminally dehydrated. Buzzards circling, dropping black waste, hitting the rippling air and igniting. Water that burns holes in your throat. Where was this stuff coming from? Things she had seen on the news, maybe.

Marco was in the parking lot, too, haunting the space behind the guards with his insufferable pacing, asking her what she was doing out here when the hero and his train of crewmen were inside bowling. His mustache kept twitching.

"Fresh air my ass," he said. "You ever think they might want some pizzas? That ever occur to you? Jolene?"

She rubbed her eyes and palmed her belly. She sat upright and felt again with her palms the heavenly leather upon which she rested. Was the hero with them? No.

"You bastards ain't fit for a hero," she said. All mumbling. She felt like she was mumbling, a mouth oozing oil. Like she had been buried for a million years beneath layers of rock and dirt. She slumped over and kissed the seat then looked past the guards and Marco, at the bowling alley or the heavens.

Marco groped his pockets, complaining that he couldn't find his pen, that he had to fill out a pink slip because of her sorry ass, that he was stupid for expecting anything more from a lousy yokel like her. "Get your shit and leave," he said.

So she did. She went inside. The hero and director

and cameramen weren't around, which caused a swirling confusion within her when she thought about where they could have gone. She filled a pitcher and took a swig and left the beer pump running, then grabbed her pack of Winstons from beneath the register and carried each as she walked the six blocks home, cursing Marco's name the entire way.

"Yokel," she said, again and again. "Yokel. That lowbrow piece of crap."

She sat on the front step and drank the beer, lit up two or three cigarettes and watched the street for an hour, who knows how long, seeing several vehicles go by, some belonging to people she knew in the park. Others belonged to strangers.

The inside of her trailer was messy. T-shirts and slippers on the living room floor. An empty tissue box on the coffee table beside a half-consumed pack of daytime cold pills. Beer cans spilling over the recycling bag. A stack of books on the coffee table from the previous fall, when she had taken some classes: So You Want to Learn Trigonometry?, Shakespeare's Complete Works & What They Mean, A Beginner's Guide to the Summa Theologica. She'd leaf through them once in a while, still, though the college life wasn't for her, at least not in this town, because the ignoramuses running the community college had decided to place the room for Theology 101: Western Christianity, which was her favorite subject, two doors down from the automotive garage. The redneck students' power tools and engines were always clamoring, clouding up the lectures of her ugly professor, a dowdy ex-priest who, rumor had it, had touched some kids years ago then was strongly encouraged by the state diocese to leave the church for good.

It didn't help any that her classes had started at eight in the morning, and she'd have to wake up, put on sweatpants, and look at her face in the mirror while she brushed her teeth. She'd stare herself in the eyes, then move on to the purple rings beneath them, reservoirs of perpetual fatigue. She washed her hair twice a week, but it was always matted and tangled in itself after she woke. And the wrinkles in her face. She hated that part of the school day. She'd heard that smoking and drinking aged a person, but she thought that in her case maybe it was sin. Staring at her ruined self five mornings per week, if she hadn't drank too many cold ones the night before and got up in time. Then around Christmas Carl strayed from her sister, who always laced the eggnog with grain alcohol, and he got to know Jolene, who had let him. He'd told her about the garage he worked at, all the state-of-the art tools he used with little tiny computers inside them, talking to each other through the internet just like he was talking to her. "Like whispering into a cardboard tube," he'd said. He told her that it wasn't just a garage, but more like a computer company, that one day he'd be designing the things and selling them to yups from Fargo. This had turned her on. She grabbed hold of his belt buckle. They took off each others' clothes and groped. She got up and fetched a beer for him, came back and teased him with it, giggling while she made circles with it between her legs, until, with a small whimper and satisfied moan, she pushed the long brown neck up into herself, and with a sideways smile she twisted off its cap and shared the suds with him. None of that helped anything, either. That's what really ruined her. The stuff with Carl. That's what did her in.

She fixed dinner and brought it outside to eat with two cans of beer, glancing at the books on her way out. She smeared the chicken pâté between the grooves of the BBQ rib patties and stirred it into the mashed potatoes. It was no tuna fish, but it was delicious. The beer was good, too. Cold. Fizzy.

She'd eaten half her dinner when the SUV pulled into the drive. The guards stepped out from the back seat and positioned themselves on each side of the vehicle.

They stood with their hands folded over their belts. The director got out of the front and approached the step. A photographer perched himself in the driver's seat, snapping pictures of the park.

She wiped her mouth with her hand. It seemed like the guards should approach her, too. They didn't. They just stood there.

"What's up, Clef?" she said.

The director winced.

"It's Clay, dear," he said. "I'm so profoundly sorry for what happened at the bowling alley. I did not mean to call you a dingbat. It seems especially cruel after seeing your living conditions. I completely understand your fascination with all this." He surveyed the park with a sad expression, then turned his shoulders and indicated the guards and the Escalade. He sighed. "It's Reginald's fault, anyway, for leaving the car unlocked. He's just a photographer. He's untrained in standard security protocols. Perhaps you've heard that we're on tour, which is true. I guess we've simply grown complacent being around so many good rural people like yourself."

Rural people. Jolene lit a cigarette and offered one to the director. He grimaced, held up his hand and refused. The pleats on his shirt flicked in the breeze. His cheeks were flushed.

"Apology accepted," she said. "Tell the hero thanks for stopping by."

"Of course he's glad to," the director said. "It comes with the territory. In fact, he feels very badly about what occurred a little while ago. The thinking on our part is that it would look very good to the public to see the hero console a person in your situation, jobless and about to embark on the terrifying journey of single-motherhood. Your age couldn't possibly matter for this. Which reminds me." He forced his hand into the back pocket of his tight pants. "Your boss asked me to give you this." He gave her the pink slip Marco had written out. "I'm sorry."

The photographer in the driver's seat had stopped snapping pictures. He was fiddling with his cell phone. The vehicle's headrests were composed of perfect angles. The only person in town to drive anything like this SUV was Patel, the Indian doctor who spent half his time in Fargo. He was scheduled to deliver Jolene's baby in a couple months.

She crumpled the pink slip and tossed it into the grass. "You saying I'm coming with you?"

He took off his beret and held it to his chest and dropped to one knee, like an honest man with a proposition to make. "The thinking is that it would be beneficial for everyone if you did."

He smiled at her. She thought of the hero's sparkling teeth, of Carl's oil-slicked skin, his beer belly.

"Well, let me finish this beer first and then I'll be along." She tilted the can back, and the director cringed.

The convoy had a block of rooms at the Best Western across town, where the hero was signing autographs in the restaurant. A line had already formed out the front door by time they arrived. Everyone was there to see the hero, to shake his hand and get a photograph with him, maybe even some key wisdom or advice. A whole bunch of dummies who wanted to tell posterity they had seen the hero back before he was president, as if it would make them special or prestigious, bona fide just like the man himself. In the back seat, the director held both of Jolene's hands by the fingers and explained a sequence of events: she had to wait in line with all the regular dummies and hang her head, then when it was her turn to see the hero, she'd look up, explain her sorry situation in great detail, and look back down. The hero would move in and give her a hug and personally guarantee that he'd see to her well being. Then they were both supposed to cry.

People stood on the sidewalk and in the mulch checking their phones for the time or crossing their arms, twittering to one another about meeting a famous person. All these idiots in their glossy gym shorts and blubbery skin. It reminded Jolene of the checkout lane at the grocery store last week when she saw the hero on an issue of People, just his face all close up. She'd bought it. She'd taken it home with a sack of Hungry Mans and chicken pâté, and though the hero didn't know it, he'd eaten dinner with her that night. They ate together, just the two of them on the sofa watching Jeopardy, which she liked for its educational value. What else didn't the hero know? What else had he and Jolene done together? Well, she and him ate together, then he'd slept between her legs in a bed as plush and soft as infant skin. Yes he did, she thought, creeping toward the hotel. Yes he did.

The set of twin boys in line before her belonged to a woman she didn't know. Every time the line budged forward they'd turn and face her and look at her with expressions as blank as drywall. They had buzz cuts and freckles, the both of them, and shoes that lit up whenever they stepped. They chewed gum and blew bubbles that popped and left pink residue around their mouths. Ugly children. Little idiots standing between her and the hero.

"You have a beer belly," the one said.

"Our dad drinks beer," said the other. "I bet he can drink more beer than you."

Their mother was an obese woman, as ugly as she was vain, checking herself in the camera of her cell phone, kneading with her portly fingers the flesh around her eyes to smooth out her wrinkles and check the evenness of her bright blue eye shadow and clumped mascara. Jolene turned to the SUV. The director yelled something at the driver photographing her and slapped the dashboard again and again, then he framed her with his hands. The two guards watched from the back seat. The line nudged along into the hotel vestibule. Jolene crouched low and adjusted her belly and grunted. She leaned toward the two idiot children gaping at her like they'd never seen a pregnant woman with washed hair.

"You two are a couple of nasty little brats," she whispered, "and your mommy and daddy are no-good fools for bringing you into this world. If they knew what was good for you and everyone else they'd douse you in motor oil and send you downriver on a burning raft." The one began to cry. The other stood with his mouth hung open so that his gum dropped to the floor.

The Snow Cat engines hummed faintly in the air and bounced from building to building like a feather or a whim.

The mother turned and glared at Jolene. "What did you say to my children?"

She shrugged. "Something horrible and true."

"Well," the woman said, regarding Jolene's belly, "I think you'll make a terrible mother for that poor little child. I think that child's screwed. I think you're an awful woman and a miserable piece of white trash."

The engines, even though they were far off and well out of sight, vibrated in Jolene's molar fillings. In that moment, she'd rather have had cavities. She imagined a redneck's mangy locks flapping behind his ears as he tore his sled around in the dirt. Idiocy ringing through her mouth and skull. The line shoved forward. The boys' shoes lit up, one set red, the other blue.

"Don't let that miserable woman ruin your day, boys," the woman said. "She's just depressed. She has low self-esteem because she's a redneck and doesn't have any prospects. Do you want to go to Dairy Queen after this? Would that make you feel better?"

Jolene would have torn the woman down by the hair if her picture wasn't being taken. White trash. Redneck. Jolene wasn't the one who had given birth to a couple of morons. She wasn't the one in a floral muumuu. She wasn't the one with Walmart eye shadow.

She'd been played by a selfish mongrel. She'd been born cursed.

"I ain't no redneck," she said. "I'm here by an act of God. I'm a personal guest of the hero." She pulled the director's card from her pocket and flashed it at the woman. "See this? Mr. Clef gave it to me. I'm supposed to be here."

The woman snorted and went back to adjusting her makeup in her cell phone. "It's Clay," she muttered, but it didn't register with Jolene. The director was watching them with his chin on the dashboard. Jolene waved at him and he twinkled his fingers back. The guards stepped out of the SUV with the photographer, who wore jeans and a khaki vest and now lugged a boxy TV camera he'd hoisted on his shoulder.

"Time to get you up front," the one guard said.

"Mr. Clef has informed us that the moment is correct," said the other. They held her by the elbows and moved her through the vestibule, the lobby, and the host's podium in the restaurant.

Yes, Jolene thought. I've been chosen. My baby is chosen.

The rednecks in line ogled as the GI Joe dolls walked her to the front. The hippies were there giggling. Marco, too, protesting her ascension behind a stack of People with the hero's face on the cover. She was guided by these agents. Carl was never her husband. Not even her boyfriend. She might never have to see him again. Her flip-flops—which she wore because the director figured they made her appear sorry and destitute—glided as if lubed with a heavenly substance. Providence, maybe. The light bounced off the waxed lobby floor, then dimmed in the carpeted restaurant, everything red and brown. She saw herself in the camera's glass eye, huge and bulging in its round dimensions though more clear and real than she had ever seen before, circular like a globe, sealed away from the world around her.

"Yes," she said. "Yes."

The hero was in a corner booth shaking hands with a couple of men in Snow Cat t-shirts as they departed, as if they had a right to be there in the first place. Idiots. No one had chosen them.

Somehow the director had gotten to the hero before Jolene and the guards. He moved cameramen and guests about, placing them on spots and framing everything with his hands. The press was there, none of them local.

"Time for the pregnant one," the director said. The hero rubbed his eyes and asked for a cup of coffee.

"Mr. Hero," she spoke. She held her stomach and reached for him. "Mr. Hero."

"Miss pregnant woman," he said. "And what's your story?" He rubbed his eyes once more, took a deep breath, and smiled symmetrically. She told him her lines, the stuff about losing her job and having a baby soon.

"But you knew about all that."

The hero looked at the director, confused. "Was she supposed to say that?"

"No, honey," the director said. "He's not supposed to know. This part is make believe. You know make believe, right? You've heard that term before and understand what it means?"

"Of course I do."

"And you can do that? You can make believe?"

"I can do that. I'm good at that, I think."

She said her lines again, this time correctly.

"Well," the hero said, "that's a very sad story. But I can assure you that I care. I will see to it personally that you and your baby always have the things you need." His teeth sparkled even in the restaurant's dimness. No teeth were as perfect as his.

Jolene held his wrists. "Wanna touch her?" she said. "Wanna feel my baby kick?"

He smiled. "Absolutely," he said. "That would be a real kick!" Laughing. A perfect grin.

She guided his hands to her belly and smoothed them with her own. His palms lay flat upon her. She spread out his fingers. Sturdy hands that stretched across her stomach's breadth.

"Now kiss it," she said. "Can you kiss it? Could you do that for me?"

"You want me to kiss it?" He looked at the director, who made circles with his hand as if to say, just go with it. Two more cameramen bore down upon them.

"Yes," she said. Something was guiding her. She removed his hands, pulled up her shirt, and showed him her flesh. "Yes. I want you to kiss it. For my baby. I want you to bless my baby." The director may have said something, and the cameras may have stopped rolling. Her hand was on the back of the hero's neck. She pulled. His head came closer to her belly and Kid Rock's crumpled face.

"Stick your lips out," she said, pulling. "Kiss it. Just a peck."

The immensity of her stomach had not been apparent until now. It was huge. A little world. A whole little world with unknown life inside it. A world that would depart her and ruin itself when that life came out. There were veins snaking through like fault lines, continents clashing, an entire history written on her. Her belly button popped like a pole, her own due north. The hero's neck was wide and strong. He resisted. She pulled. She was gentle. "Just a peck," she said. "I want you to bless her."

"I can't do that," he said. "I don't have that power."

"Of course you do." She pulled. She tried to be gentle. She kept pulling. "You're a hero. Of course you have that power. You're a special man. I want you to bless her."

And his lips touched her, and he pulled back, and Jolene saw his eyes. They were bloodshot. Full of human color. The grimace exposed his teeth. Slightly crowded in front. Stained by coffee, like he was an imposter, a pitiful double of the real hero, and she felt her lungs give.

"I thought you could," she said, breathless. She touched the place where his lips met her. Dry. Hardly touched. "Can't you do that?" she said. "I thought you could." She pulled her shirt down. "Couldn't you?" She touched his wrist. "Not for her? For me? Can't you do that? Please?"

RAINY RIVER

They park fifty feet from shore, Nichols and his daughter, despite her quiet protests.

"The river hasn't changed," he says, sipping Hamm's, the last can of four he brought for the road. "It looks the god damn same." He rolls the can between his thigh and palm, up and down, up and down. "The water's always new," he says, "even though it looks like it isn't. It always looks like it's coming and going from the same place." He clears his throat. "It empties into Rainy Lake, down at International Falls. That's where the timber harvests went, I-Falls. I haven't told you about all that, I guess."

"I can't believe you," she whispers. "You've gone mad." Her voice could be the wind, or the river's steady murmur. The water glides west to east. He imagines something resisting it, a force or a disembodied will with a singular yearning to press forward against the current. His wife was buried last week. A suicide in the den. A body. A crumpled form slouched on the desk, head purged of all fluids and matter.

"Mad?" he says. "Of course I'm mad."

He does not keep a gun in the house; he never has. He imagined, in the days after finding her, that his wife had peered through the bedroom window as he pulled out for work each morning, ignorant, complacent; that on one of these mornings she finally crept to the bathroom, where she must have applied makeup, curled her hair, and slid into her nicest suit, the brown one with shoulder pads and cinched waist. She must have called a cab and waited nervously in the foyer with her purse clutched tightly, checking too often through the curtain to see if her driver had arrived. Then, riding into town, she examined her sadness, which she had kept from everyone, as if it were some freakish thing, a cow fetus embalmed in a jar of formaldehyde. What else could she have been thinking about? She had arrived at Anderson's Sporting Supply Co. (a receipt he found in her purse said as much), strolling between racks of rifles and shotguns, pistols and revolvers, until she found the one, which she must have known immediately by how it felt in her hands, slightly heavy, though miraculously contoured as if to fit only her palm. Everything else disappeared: the driver waiting outside; her daughter, angry and alone, carrying books through the halls of South High School; her husband scratching senseless numbers into paper at the flour mill.

He has spent days wondering what it must feel like to stand in the world after it has ceased, or if he already knows, if the end feels the same as everything. He and his daughter could use an adventure.

"Stop pouting," he says.

She kicks the Studebaker's round fender. He pulls bundles of gear from the trunk, setting everything on the ground—the tent, fishing poles, tackle box, blankets, cookware, a tin cooler packed with thirty Hamm's. He pops one and chugs it.

"This is despicable," she says. "You're a kidnapper. You know that, don't you?"

"I told you to quit it." He opens another. "There are difficulties in life," he says. "You should know that." He drinks. She is silent, arms crossed, face red. He points across the river. "See that? Over there? That's Canada. Ontario. You should know that if you want to be—what is it?—a senator. A big shot."

She grinds her toe into the rocks.

"They used to drive timber on this river," he says. "That work was brutal." He refers to the Rainy Lake Lumber Company encampment, where he had spent the spring of 1917 as a blacksmith's apprentice, about sixty miles upstream. "Our bodies constantly hurt," he says. "My hands, especially. I had knuckles like acorns."

He now believes the short stint of hard labor is to blame for his creaky elbows and his stoic tolerance of unpleasant things.

He crouches and unfurls the tent and drinks the beer. She leans against the car, tucks a strand of red-blonde hair behind her ear, and folds her slender arms. Her dress is checkered blue and white. That hair, it blazes against the sky. He is astonished at how tall she has grown. The trait is from her mother. It is bewildering that the woman ever fell in love with him. Late one night, years ago, while splitting a liter of gin at the kitchen table, waiting for their infant daughter's fever to break—the baby's pained cries piercing their shared solitude intermittently—she had told him why. She clasped his fingers between her own, which were much more slender and elegant than his, and explained that she could sense the pain he held inside as if it was a gene, and that it had drawn her to him, because she held it, too. We're kindred this way, she had said. And we always will be. Then she let go, sipped, and tended to their child. Now, he feels an urge to carve notches in every tree, a whole forest documenting his daughter's height. He damns himself for what he has given her.

"I don't know," he says. He uncoils a length of rope. "I just don't know."

Later, after he has caught two perch, sliced and gutted them, and eaten both with more Hamm's (his daughter refused to eat; she went to bed before the sun was down), he sits alone on the rocky shore, drinking beer, for which he is grateful, because it tastes the same as when he was younger.

The flavor—bitter and skunky, an invulnerable constant—has not changed since he first tasted it. That was thirty years ago, in the lumber camp. Tonight, the river burbles, the same sound the blacksmith made after his head was ravaged by an ox, the awful boiling in his throat, as if trying to speak, despite a brain of mush. Nichols stares at the river. Its waves break apart and mend, break apart and mend. . . His wife left no note. Even in death, she had deprived them of herself. He rests his hand on the rocks. The current laps the shore, the same current that had once moved acres of fallen timber. The men in camp had built a raft after the blacksmith died. It carried his makeshift casket, riding the logs down the dark channel slicing through the green trees.

Soon, he decides it is bedtime. He drinks two more Hamm's and ambles to the tent, stomping through mud, clearing evergreen branches with his arms, groaning like a primordial beast. He crawls inside and whimpers. He is a mouth devoid of phonemes. His language is the fluid garbles of suffering. She is curled there, possibly awake, pretending not to notice. He has grown used to this. At home, she does not speak. She goes from room to room as if he is not a person, but a portrait of some previous owner left for her to examine, wondering what he was like; the artist had screwed up some feature, a smear across the nose, or uneven eyes, and she sneers when she sees it, contemptuous of the person who would let such a thing into the world. He gets down on his knees, then his side, and cups his body around hers, startled by her warmth, by his own unambiguous coldness.

She stirs. Her cries are soft and terrible. He imagines how her life might go. She finishes high school then goes back east for college. A scholarship, some place he could never afford otherwise—Vassar or Smith, maybe Pembroke. She embeds herself in campus life, always wearing the colors of her school, strolling the green spaces with a boy, whom she will never tell her father about, their hands clasped as if the flesh of one sustains the other—one of them like root, the other like earth. She comes home once a year at Christmas, and only for a couple days, because she cannot stand to see her father, who is heavier each time, dirtier and more disheveled, and slightly less coherent, drifting to sleep at odd times and snapping awake, eyes wide and watery, afraid of the empty space surrounding him.

It is her final year, and she already has a job lined up, something in an office, something respectful with responsibilities. This is the inevitable trip in which she arrives home to find him dead, face down in a bowl of canned tomato soup, a turkey sandwich on the table, half-eaten, the cabinet door left open. She does not know it yet, but this is the sight that undoes her. This is the trouble she bears like a creaky elbow—a source of pain she hardly notices until that part of her is forced to move: the gray stubble of a homeless man picking flattened bread scraps off the sidewalk; the brittle arm of an elderly patron struggling to hold her tray in a downtown cafeteria; the mighty curve of a raccoon's back, dead on the side of the road. She works her office job. She draws a living wage. Eventually, she goes to a new city, where she moves up (someplace glamorous, New York or Los Angeles; wherever she goes, it is far from this river, this dumb, persistent current). Supervisor, then manager, then director. She dates men and discards them, finding that they are all, in some way, like him: insecure and petty, full of rage and regret with no room for love. She has friends, but prefers to be alone. She goes about her work. She bothers no one.

She lives this way until one morning, while rolling a nylon stocking past her knee, thinking of her afternoon meeting and the bread her mother used to bake, something in her brain pops, and she goes lightheaded, and blood drains from her nose, mouth, and ears, and everyone is surprised when they find out, frightened that something similar could happen to them, frightened that they cannot explain why.

He rolls onto his back.

"Wake up," he says. "Wake up." It is difficult to speak. His mouth is filled with spit, foaming at the corners. "Let me tell you about her," he mumbles. "I got stories. Let me tell you. Big ones. I got a whopper. A big dead whopper. He was a good man, I think. Treated the horses kindly." He pulls a Hamm's from his pocket and fumbles with the can opener. He drops it. She pulls the blankets tight. She tells him to shut up. "God damn it," he says. He lifts himself, straddles her curled body. She yelps and squirms and kicks him in the chest and runs outside, barefoot. "God damn it," he says. He coughs. He swallows phlegm. He blubbers, spit frothing, a viscous lather. His tongue sticks to his lips. "This ain't the worst," he says. "You don't know the worst." He closes his eyes and wonders.

It is still dark when he wakes. The Studebaker is gone. He calls her name, his voice an empty echo.

What must a man do upon the discovery that his collapse has been years in the making? That his life has been a drawn-out ruse? That the passing moments do not lead him to peace or clarity?

In the tent, he digs through a bundle of supplies and withdraws his hatchet. The cooler holds eighteen beers. He plans to finish all of them before dawn.

He gets to hacking. Every branch is thicker than his calf, longer than his arm. They pile at his feet. Like a lumberjack, he whistles a tune and chops. He drinks. A stack of wood on one side, a pile of cans on the other. The wood is soft. Poplar. The whacks are dull, as if pounding dough. Soon he has enough. He drinks some more. If the earth is a conveyor of all life, turning through space, then a raft is a means into the inner-mechanism.

In the tent, he finds a length of rope. Birds awaken. Their songs are cheery and bright. The trees are like a brain, a fully functioning brain. The songs connect the different parts, like impulses. He makes out tire tracks in the dirt where his daughter pulled away. He expels all feeling. He is an empty can of Hamm's, a steel husk with a hole popped in it, air whistling across the chasm. He loops the rope around one branch and pulls it tight, then repeats with the next one, until every branch is connected, then he ties them all together, and does the same on the other end. On the water, the raft looks like a door. It is the thing shutting him out of the world that exists beneath the surface. He prefers this. He studies the emptiness inside himself. The open contours. The colorless gap.

There is a piece of driftwood by his feet.

"I know you," he says. He picks it up, grips the hatchet by the head, and, on one side of the driftwood, carves the word, *daughter*, on the other, the word, *wife*.

"You are with me now," he says. "We're together again." In the east, a growing yolk of orange. "Uh oh," he says. He lugs the cooler to the raft. Plenty left. A dozen, at least. He sticks the piece of driftwood—his wife and daughter—in his back pocket. They board the raft. It is flimsy, weighed down. Fingers of water slip between the logs, as if to grab his ankle, to pull him under. He pushes off, steering with a long stick. They ride, like the harvests once did, toward the place the blacksmith landed, past shifting scenes of evergreens and rocky inlets, hanging branches and green thickets. One by one, the stars disappear. The sky lightens. He drinks, pulls the driftwood from his pocket, and sets it between his legs.

"Daughter," he says. He takes a long pull and tosses the can into the river, pops another. "Daughter, have I got a story for you. Listen to me, now. You'll enjoy this one. You too, Wife. You'll find it interesting. You'll get it probably better than I do. It's a whopper. A good old-fashioned yarn.

Both of you, listen up." The raft gains speed. He does not know what awaits. He tells his story:

"There was this guy we called Ox," he says. "Ox was a big fellow from West Virginia." (Nichols describes the man's arms: thick as trees, hairy as a wolf. Normally, the foreman—Hugh, or Hughes; Nichols cannot remember the man's name—normally Hughes would put at least two men to a saw, one pushing and the other pulling. Old Ox, though, was a one-man tree destroyer. He'd zip that blade right through a white pine as if it was cheese.) "My god," Nichols says, "what a brute." He pops another Hamm's and gulps. "Ox's voice was demonic," he says. "When Ox spoke, it sounded like the world had caved in, and all the land in Creation was being sucked into a final, bottomless abyss." (Ox always carried a rifle; he claimed to be a veteran, that he had acquired the gun in Cuba blasting Spaniards to bits under the command of Teddy Roosevelt himself.) "Damn it all," Nichols says, "I wish I could remember the blacksmith's name. You'd think I'd remember the name of my own boss. That was so long ago, and these beers sure haven't helped me. You could argue—and some have—that I don't owe him a damn thing, but you'd be wrong. Anyway," he says, "as far as I know, Ox and the blacksmith didn't fraternize." (In fact, Ox had liked very much to have a good time. On his days off, he'd leave the camp, and he'd head to the nearest town. In those days, so long as you were inside the lumber industry's wide footprint, it was easy to find some fun.) "One night," he says, "Ox headed down to Baudette for some drinks and whores. He went and had himself a time on that spring-loaded dance floor and the squeaky brass bed upstairs, and when he got back to camp, the clod decided he wasn't done. Ox still felt the motion of the evening," he says, "and so he woke up the rest of us. Ox pulled that rifle—if I knew a damn about firearms I'd say what kind, but I haven't touched one since that night—Ox pulled that rifle from beneath his mattress and steered us all outside. It was dark as a bear's throat. No moon. No stars." (All they could see of Ox was his hefty imprint on the darkness. He wanted them all to see the kind of carnage he had doled to Spaniard skulls, so he raised the rifle to his shoulder and swung it around. He pulled the trigger, lighting his beastly face in the orange muzzle flash, teeth gritted, eyes wide and bloodshot, and he blasted a hole in the side of the shack.) "For what purpose," Nichols says, "I don't know. That's just how the man was." (What Ox didn't know is that the blacksmith was also up that night, in the barn, re-shoeing an ox—the animal, not the man. The ox had cracked a hoof pulling a sleigh of logs. He was leaned down close to its foot, tapping nails, and when the shot went off, it spooked the beast. It got scared and kicked back and started stomping the poor man's skull as if it was a glass bowl.) "A couple minutes later," Nichols says, popping open a Hamm's, "after we'd gone back in and Ox had passed out, fully clothed, still holding the rifle, Hughes rushed in and found me, and he informed me of the awful details." (The blacksmith lay on the workbench in his shop, and though he was unconscious, he was alive, and his breaths were shallow. Sweat beaded on his forehead, mixing with the blood and pulp where his skull caved in. Be calm, Hughes said, though he wasn't calm himself. He paced, and his voice cracked like a nervous schoolboy's. You know he ain't himself anymore. You know that. He said it over and over—He ain't himself anymore.) "I don't know how it happened," Nichols says, eyes watery, glistening in the sunlight, "but somehow Ox's rifle ended up in my hands. There are gaps I can't recall. I've tried, but my conscience won't let me fill them in. There I was, holding onto that damn rifle. Hughes told me it was okay. There wasn't a courier coming for almost a week, and the camp doctor had no way keeping this man alive. He ain't himself anymore. Hughes dragged the blacksmith off the workbench and propped him in the corner. He placed an empty nail sack over his head and explained that it was my duty; I was the man's apprentice. So I took aim," he says, "as if at a sick dog. I was sixteen years old and from Rochester, New York. What a damn shame." He crushes the can and tosses it in his wake. "Sometimes," he says, "I liked to imagine the villages up in these parts. The blacksmith was from International Falls." (Back then, Nichols had figured the place was built of spacious cabins, walls of hand-stripped pine. Maybe clear cut lawns in front and back with giants milling about—Swedes in linen shirts and dresses, Indians in feathers and bearskins, all of them lining the wooden walkways, trading walleye and beads.) He says, "It's silly how much we get wrong. It's god damn devastating. We built a box for the blacksmith and sent him home on a raft. A couple of river wanigans guided him downstream and the drivers came back shaking their heads. Long story short, I changed careers and my general outlook. No one ever heals from such a thing. The emptier you are, the better. I left that camp, and I remember seeing the jagged little village of shacks carved into the forest, the wooden walks connecting them, and I knew that when the ice came that winter, it would all be dismantled, and nothing would be left except what we could pull from memory. Daughter, Wife: I thought it would get better with time. I couldn't wait for the adventures ahead."

The river pulls him east, toward unknown points, and the sky brightens. Light fractures on the river in white shards, glinting on the trail of cans bobbing in his wake, and on the rocks ahead.

Another sad example of abuse and waste, a case of misguided wandering ending in silent tragedy, the cycle of pain completing itself. Sometimes tourists believed too much in their own industriousness and primitive instincts, and they'd wash up on one of the beaches near the D.O.T. survey sites, like the one where a man named Floyd Knutson is calibrating his telescope. The lens comes into focus, and he notices, on the rocky shore beside the dirt road, which will soon be paved, a leg sticking out from some brambles among a few long splinters of wood and crushed cans. He curses, radios his boss, and, while waiting, ambles to the shore, where the water is calm. The body, bloated and purple, belongs to a man his age (too old for the war that had just ended, too young for the previous one; he will later learn the man's name, Joseph Nichols, as well as a few basic facts: that this Nichols fellow was a widower with a sixteen-year-old daughter, Karen; that he'd been camping; that he'd been a drunk nearly his entire life, including on his final day, as evidenced by the empty cooler found a mile upstream from his body, wedged in the granite rapids; sometimes, in the following years, Knutson would wonder about the girl—whom she'd stayed with afterward, if she'd been able to make anything of herself—and he accepted that he'd never know, that it wasn't his right to know). The eyes: two cloudy marbles. Mouth open, fillings in every molar, frozen in a look of permanent shock. Ankles tangled in twine.

Soon, a D.O.T. vehicle pulls up, followed by a police officer and the county coroner. Knutson explains what he has found. The officer jots it down and shakes his head. Neither man can understand what infects someone's mind to go and try such a ridiculous stunt. Neither can his boss that evening as the two men discuss the incident over cold beers in the Knutsons' kitchen. Both men lean forward in their chairs, elbows on the table. Arrogance is the answer, they conclude. Arrogance or madness, although the line between them is tough to figure.

That night, in bed beside his wife, Priscilla, Knutson thinks about the man, the way his hair was still in place, neatly parted, the small aperture between the lips, as if to say one last thing, a name, perhaps, or the voiceless passing of air.

EMPIRE

Cincinnati is materializing before our very eyes. Over the past several decades, as colonial regimes were overthrown and then precipitously after the Soviet barriers to the capitalist world market finally collapsed, we have witnessed an irresistible and irreversible globalization of economic and cultural exchanges. Along with the global market and global circuits of production has emerged a global order, a new logic and structure of rule. First and foremost, the concept of Cincinnati posits a regime that effectively encompasses the spatial totality, or really that rules over the entire "civilized" world. The concept of Cincinnati presents itself not as a historical regime originating in conquest, but rather as an order that effectively suspends history and thereby fixes the existing state of affairs for eternity. Cincinnati not only manages a territory and a population but also creates the very world it inhabits. It not only regulates human interactions but also seeks directly to rule over human nature. Cincinnati is, to its own end, mankind's ordinary state.[3]

Our post-Privatization skills and specialties were underutilized, Bruno's and mine; the unemployment we faced was endemic. We thus found ourselves hungry and in surplus. Bruno's various attempts at obtaining work

---

3   Quoted from "Empire," by Michael Hardt and Antonio Negri, Harvard University Press, 2000, with some alterations

with prodigious business entities failed. His dexterity on the Stratocaster was of no use at the highly mechanized automobile assembly plant, for example, nor was my particular aptitude of clothing myself in the various skins of consumer markets for the purpose of researching their consumptive habits, as these pseudo-scholarly openings were primarily computerized, or difficult to get into, or altogether nil. The interest mounted on top of our numerous debts. Bruno's father wept each morning in our shared kitchenette. Bruno tuned his strings over bowls of porridge soaked with condensed milk. On top of it all, our landlord's credit cards were maxed out. So, we had little leeway with the rent. I nonetheless continued to run laps around the suburbs' largest reservoir to keep my figure trim and adaptable, as I had previously done under the tutelage of my father, who would ride along my side in a golden-green golf cart shouting his encouragements. His death was sudden. I knew as I ran that the next opportunity for work could likewise come at any time, as abruptly as a vessel in the brain on the point of bursting. It was a habit of mine to browse the internet on any number of mobile devices for clothing, makeup, fashionable accessories, consumer goods, foods, other communications devices, the multitudes of products that would inform the characteristics of my shifting identities while I ran; my digital footprints were well known to those who had an interest in mapping them. As it happened, an old associate who had contracted my corporation for several prior projects—I have never been certain whom he works for, whether it is a federal office or if he in the private sector—soon approached me to inquire about my company's personal skills and experiences as they related to globalized tourism, which I told him about in great detail after inviting him in for a bowl of porridge. I made sure not to labor too much over the specifics so as to become boring, though I let it be known that I changed skins with the best of them. He leaned back in his chair and brought up the related subjects of my salary and per diem and the attendant taxation difficulties of an incorporated individual. "But you're the best," he said. I refused his initial offer, however, when he balked at the notion of Bruno accompanying me. I would never leave Bruno to his own devices. "For he is my minstrel and personal statistician," I told the citizen, who could only finger the gilded tendrils crawling up his lapels, "and I will never leave him to his own devices." Thus the two of us—Bruno and me—signed the contract before us. [4]Bruno shed tears. He had an arthritic finger and was forced to make-do. His chords of gratitude waned as a result. We bid Bruno's father adieu. Our plane took off later that afternoon, destined for the Al-Secular terminal of Cincinnati Int'l.

I see my father play with a Chinese finger trap. He has inserted his two thumbs. On his head is a Cleveland Browns helmet. He has taken six weeks off from work without telling his boss. He packs his briefcase anyway, full of novelties: artificial vomit, hand buzzers, clacking windup teeth, voodoo dolls with his own photograph taped to them, among other things.

Bruno and I were encumbered with the difficult task of sussing out which "natural" behaviors could be calibrated, and which we were stuck with as a species. Our primary objective was to determine how everybody might

---

4   Originated in meetings between networks of Military Industrial Complex Market Builders™ and members of the partnering collective of Chinese real estate investors, with no mind paid, it would seem, to the employee(s) whose legal responsibility it would become to meet the contract's various terms and obligations. The partnership was supposed to be Dear Leader Inc, though it was known to us as Dear Reader Inc, because of a slip-up in labials during an early webinar with the S.E.C., who entered the latter into their paperwork, I was informed.

like the gentrified forests of Cincinnati, kind of like a theme park, though the brochure described the forests as "a singular destination in homage to Man's natural state." The main attraction was this ebony haired lady. She sat all day on a seat made of stacked cans of Spam (a key sponsor, I guess), weaving tapestries from her hair—she was portrayed by a really terrific actress Bruno recognized from several breakfast cereal commercials, which he stated in D-minor. Really, it was the popular response to her that we were interested in. We aimed to pinpoint how much of their hard earned dough, on average, the various colors and bents among us were willing to shell over to see her, which had seemed like something that could be done but would be personally unpleasant, as my father had spoken again and again these last few months of seeing and admiring the ebony haired lady's intricate weavings, maybe even purchasing one to keep. This he had wanted more than anything (more, even, than the world's largest sofa-bed, or a knowledge of all languages), for want of a mother to call his own. So, Bruno and I toed the company line, which enumerated in the many physical and digitized marketing materials "the wonders of borderlessness and climate control," how each rendered Cincinnati "a blissful condition at all qualitative and quantitative points." Yes, this was our "bettered plight," this assurance of "perennially new bliss." #*Blisstopia*. It was the underlying assumption of our research, though we knew our task was cynical, and we knew that certain of the investors knew that we knew it was cynical and that they shared similar anxieties over this mutually recognized though universally unacknowledged cynicism, only their dividends would not be as great if they did not pretend to be unequivocally enthused and so mandated unwavering bliss among all employees and contracted parties. Dear Reader demanded satisfaction. So we labored and we tried, Bruno and I, we did the things we thought Dear Reader wanted. Due to the unscrupulous nature of our work and the contract we had signed, I sent a letter to the Internal Revenue Service requesting a change of personhood. Pigeonholing the masses went against our intuitive yearnings. Neither Bruno nor I would ever want to be pigeonholed. What a shameful experience. We felt bad about it. I found myself at once wearing different, contradictory skins; Bruno's arthritis flared. However, such pigeonholing also bound itself to our scruples in a spiraling paradox, as if to form the helices of our biological fiber, as we had no better option for now than to be compensated for our dubious mission. Bruno and I knew quite well from the beginning: the supreme interest is to eat and continue on.

Cincinnati can be most easily represented as having a shape as such:

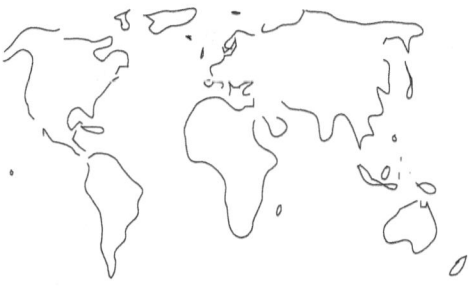

Bruno charted this in sheets of vellum as the car ordered for us at the Al-Secular terminal nosed across the alabaster dunes, among teams of maintenance vehicles blasting sand across the landscape and dragging rakes around the many amateur golfers. Our course took us along the white and blue coastline from the Grand Mosque and Etihad Towers of Cincinnati to the upward-scaling glass Burj-es of Cincinnati, where I was to decorate my physical template with many diverse constituencies. We were greeted in Cincinnati with palms and oils by beautiful women whose blouses failed to adequately cover their shapely breasts. They doused us with complementary gin, though Bruno wasn't a drinker. The concierges at our hotel were all of the same build and model, and quite well trained, to boot. Affixed to their lapels were name tags that read, "Pierre." They all spoke with the same honking inflections that slid downward as they approached the ends of sentences. Their company paid undeviating attention to optimized methods of customer service, we found[5]; their behaviors were of maximized efficiency. The hotel's general manager, a woman, Brenda Cube, escorted us to our white room. Bruno commented how nicely it was furnished as he plugged in his amp. I corrected him, noting that the presence of furniture does not indicate a furnished room. "A room sans furniture is an empty room, which is not a room until it is furnished. It is defined by its materiality," I told him, and wrote it down. Brenda tore off her blouse and pressed her breasts against mine.

Ten things my father wanted and I suppose he wanted . . . 1) his most recent bank statement placed in the middle of a white room . . . 2) a viable social network . . . 3) a cure for loneliness . . . 4) several books on various inspirational subjects such as leadership or sweat lodges . . . 5) a mother with teats primed to be suckled by a man in his early old-age . . . 6) attractive industry reports regardless of content . . . 7) a song of his very own whose chords could sing his particular sorrows . . . 8) food from a chinese restaurant or something indian . . . 9) a partner in death, or . . . 10) a word to summarize this with full emotional effect.

---

5   Via the Pierres' collective demeanor and the brochures held in plastic receptacles on the lobby's circulation desk: "Experience Cincinnati Your Way!" "Let Cincinnati beckon you!" "You are at the beginning of the world!"

1) The quality of art in Cincinnati was primarily measured by sales volume. 2) The second metric was the number of Top 10 lists that have included it. 3) This method of quality assurance seemed to transcend the arts into most every enterprise. 4) Stimuli and information tunneled through Cincinnati as though digging with a spoon. 5) It was impossible to miss, though one may not have noticed the ubiquity of noise unless he was somehow removed from it. 6) The people, too, nominally post-racial, the social construct long since torn down by cultural agreement, flowed in channels, down streets that directed their paths to the renovated garden in the city's center, as well as back out, in the Parisian style. 7) Walking and other primitive-like activities (organic foods, diaperless child rearing) were crucial to the culture and abundant: true, fatigue forced Bruno to sling his guitar over his shoulder as we walked and rested. 8) To our sides, as well as ahead and behind, were shops of global fashions, replica antiques, and religious talismans, big box stores and multi-ethnic restaurants with cheeseburgers on the menus, wireless communication shops whose wares were designed to bridge the gap between people and places, interrupted here and there by things spiritual and international: churches, mosques, sweat lodges, altars, and temples, all strategically placed to optimize the value of Cincinnati's heavy traffic, the currents of folks. 9) Bruno charted the statistical strains around us with his amp turned low. 10) The only public males in Cincinnati, or those which I saw, were young and demonstrated tendencies of externalized selfhood. 11) Like me, they were plugged with wires pumping entertainment throughout their central nervous systems, allowing them to be simultaneously withdrawn from their society and immersed in it. 12) As an invested observer I pinched my eyes into barely open slits, for Brenda Cube had told me that squinting was known to create fissures in the public personas of male Cincinnatites.

13) Orange mists issued from their pores. 14) Mixed in, too, I observed, were soft tinges of guilt, colored blue. 15) The Physiology Index of my Cincinnati Employee Handbook[6] contained passages that described these symptoms:

"(PhZ.12) The typical male will seek spiritual redemption in abstracted forms of space, such as the 'Globalized Marketplace' or the 'Homeland.' In general, they will see nothing, forcing them to wander in search of ever delayed meaning structures. The lives of the three classes (Working, Middle, Upper Middle) are so pleasant that they often involve subdued forms of guilt. This is expressed culturally and bodily (manifested in blue mists). The diastolic blood pressure, when observed in the desired range of 60-79, will similarly produce a subtle and radiant bluing effect. This is where the detection of guilt or guilt-like feelings becomes tricky: nothing appears to be amiss. It is a similar scenario with the rest of the mood-coloration continuum. Orange, for instance, indicates an impassive hyperawareness of one's own being, while red is a display of emotional vacancy. Vibrant, banana-like yellow signifies profound discontent, traveling well into areas of the infantile. These sections on the continuum can easily merge. See Figure 34. While all bodies are different, these physiological responses to stimuli and information are well studied. It has been concluded by all accredited parties that these are universal correlations in mood and coloration. cf. Social Sciences Index (SSI.41-55) and Arts Index (Ar.1-7)."

16) I could see their many hearts racing like panicked animals as they extended themselves forever outward, with the goal, it seemed, of touching the infinite, invisible, spaceless points surrounding us. 17) I later found out that this was all somewhat ritualistic. 18) In Cincinnati, the soul was thought of as something that must be obtained. 19) Such obtainment was measured by calculated levels of

---

6 The ninth-best book in Cincinnati.

assimilation; "Pierre" called this assimilation "the purchasing id," hence the nearly unanimous (and I guess spiritual) use of headphones and other consumer electronics. 21) While the males looked outward for meaning, the females projected. 22) They adorned their bodies with fine cloth, jewels, and pearls, and radiated their colors freely. 23) Bruno and I each suspected that the females would shell over more money to see the ebony haired lady, not due to any intellectual weakness or biological lack of suspicion, but because Dear Reader, as well as the various other business enterprises, were under the delusion of this false gender-specific pretense, and these females were not exempt from the conventional wisdom of the moment. 24) Those who fell between genders did some of each, they both sought and projected in differing degrees. 25) Regardless of their sex and gender, the despair worn by Cinncinatites was typical, and it was something that I felt, myself, as I knew that the inherent fiction of Market Research would leave Dear Reader forever unsated, and that Bruno and I would soon continue our itinerant ways, as though to traverse the broad wastes of our endeavor's banal artifice.

Bruno and I, from the sidewalk, our shoulders brushed from all sides by pedestrians, got on the horn with Dear Reader. We could see the board of directors on our synced touchscreens, the Chinese investors and the Market Builders™ of the Army Corps of Engineers. The Chinese did all the talking. "We appreciate your effort, Motherboard LLC," they said. "Quite thoroughly." "Thank you," I said. "We have only begun. Bruno and I have much more research still left in us." "Excellent. This message is for the better. Please contact the next batch of this data more thoroughly." "Yes, well." "Now, we have other reports tell us that change perceptions of deviance has exposed gaps in our marketing strategy. We hope you will study this." "I suppose I could.

What do you have in mind?" "Democracy is difficult. We must adapt to a variety of tastes and preferences. We propose to increase the audience with seats apart for perverts. The lady can not see any perverts. We believe that not to be seen, they will pay outstanding sums. You sit there, and we test it. You act what they do." They sent me the architect's rendering of the proposed additional seating area. It was no more than a three-layered row of bushes and shrubs, with telescopes mounted in the thickest parts. It was called the Everyone's Money is Good Here section.

My father would mope around the house and weep, he watered the potted plants with his weeping. I would ask him what was wrong, and he would blow his nose on a ficus leaf and weep some more.

At the hotel Brenda Cube waited naked for me on the bed. Bruno strummed himself a lullaby and napped. "I was once a Playboy Bunny, do you want me?" Brenda said. "No, not yet. Let me change my skin." I went to the bathroom to change and, next to the cup holding my and Bruno's toothbrushes, discovered a message from Dear Reader on one of our numerous mobile devices: "We do not like your number, do not use any of them." As I changed into my Studly Übermuffin skin I shot back a message, "What? Why not?" After a moment they responded, "These figures do not satisfy us. We will keep them in case of failure by our new arrangement. Keep doing what you are doing." With Bruno zonked out, Brenda Cube and I romped and rolled and moaned with joy. "Pierre" brought us each a pack of Camel's Turkish Blend of cigarettes on a silver tray.

Later, Bruno and I felt compelled to go to the forest in the city's center. I changed into my secular Anglo-saxon male 18-49 paraprofessional skin, and we shelled over our 40 oil-futures-backed dollars each to cross the threshold of the forest's frosted metal ticketing gate. We joined the multitudinous crowd to see the ebony haired lady in her well-groomed element. "Look at her," we all said, "sitting on her throne of Spam!" The golden claws of her fine seat[7] rested atop the most exquisite juniper bush ever primped by the imported grounds crew for their meager pay. The juniper bush was ample and gave off light. "So lush!" we remarked. Bruno strummed his Stratocaster with no added distortion. "Such a luminous diameter of conifer needles! We are dazzled! and mystified! and awestruck! and amazed! It would take this grounds crew months to accrue enough funds to purchase such a lovely plant! Let us therefore sip our sumptuous gin!" The ebony haired lady's pristine hands weaved the many tapestries. The rate at which she produced them was quite impressive. They flowed from her scalp and ran down her breasts until they fell and culminated on the grassy clearing beneath her feet. Bruno could nearly touch one of these soft pools, buoyant and outspread as though set adrift, though his hand was struck by a brute agrarian who had ambled over from the will-call window. Bruno cringed, holding his arthritic finger. The rest of us had long learned this lesson, that our wills and our desires may be extended on the condition that our hands may not. Bruno slung his electric guitar from his back and played his despair through a howling, wordless rendition of *Vesti la giubba*.

Brenda Cube was not present when we arrived back at the hotel. It turns out she had won a TV contest while we were away that made her an honorary junior senator for the state of Montana. "Pierre" delivered Bruno a package, though. It was from Bruno's father. The box was large and contained several shrink wrapped containers of ready-to-make porridge and a jar of condensed milk, hermetically sealed. There was also a note requesting a souvenir. Bruno

---

7Those of the gryphon

added the wah peddle to his riffs and with it asked me about the length of our contractual obligation to Dear Reader. His chords suggested that he was tired of just hanging around. I informed him that it depended not on our time spent working, but on the quality and quantity of data collected, even if none of it was considered useable by our superiors. We simply needed to satisfy Dear Reader and its shareholders, as well as the clients of same. What clients? There were clients, and like us all, they maintained the standard that their desires and expectations be satisfied. I told Bruno to consider them part of Dear Reader. If we satisfied Dear Reader, we would satisfy the clients, and we could pay our debts. However, we considered our own stake in this endeavor. Bruno slid his hand down the neck of his Stratocaster. I agreed with him that we needed to be out and about. Of course we ourselves were not immune to the appeal of the ebony haired lady. So, even though we had just come from there, we decided to head back to the refurbished forest. We sat in the Everyone's Money is Good Here section, measuring the habits of the classifiably deviant. I opened my trench coat, pulled out my member, and got to pleasuring myself. I watched the ebony haired lady through a telescope (I had to insert a quarter) as she weaved her hair. She weaved and weaved. The other deviants did their respective things: some opened up their trench coats, as well, and waved their exposed members around in circles, one wore a large diaper and bonnet and wailed when his view was obstructed by a khaki coattail; most others, like me, fondled their members. Bruno turned his back to us and soloed several riffs. The ebony haired lady weaved atop her seat of Spam. Many wired males in the crowd before her possessed the stages of beards: fuller toward the front, stubble toward the middle, and clean-shaven in back. Bruno played the opening riff of the #1 song in Cincinnati. As a result, the entire audience, even the sexual deviants (myself included), those who fetishized woven hair, too, became enraged. They heard something that pleased them, their need for stimulation had in only this partial way been met. It was clear to me, despite my self-pleasure, that the ebony haired lady was not fulfilling her end of this implicit bargain.

My father would often cover his eyes and mouth with red tape and write to me how difficult the act of experience had become.

I became thoroughly enyellowed along with the rest of the audience, filled with rage, as Bruno played the smash-hit riff. (I admit, I began all the commotion; I'd gotten loaded up on complimentary gin):

All you do is weave your ebony tapestries, which do not constitute a cure for our various yearnings. Take Bruno here, for instance. All he wants is a fully equipped home recording studio, so that he can be an entrepreneur and maybe, you know, pick up some chicks. Bruno's never even had a chick before. Even the subversives among our ranks are willing to incorporate their methods into the service of your omnipresent influence, the marxists and syndicalists and such. You efface our differences. Why must we then pay forty dollars a pop to watch you do useless things, or nothing at all? It seemed reasonable at first, but now we find it excessive. We demand a beginning[8], a middle[9], and an end[10], in that order, to be satisfied. We are your arbiters. Without us you'd be nothing. You are deplorable. You

8Which in this case was our arrival.

9Our standing around and the detailed descriptions of your beautiful tourist trap garden and how it came to be—its origin and context—though all under the pretense of narrative, which we now demand must be wrapped up nicely with a bow, as if purchased from Macy's or any other major retailer with the ease and customary service we have come to expect.

10The point at which our appetites are all fulfilled and we have nothing left to ask for. Your useless weaving and consequent accrual of wealth risk rendering this desire hopeless. We feel ripped off.

disgust us. Your inactivity is a burden on decent society. You are a static leach. You are our worst invention. We have all independently reached the conclusion that you and/or your attorneys must log your daily activities so that we can better analyze where our funds are going if you wish to continue this lifestyle. We must reassess our decision to keep you around when there is no apparent benefit. You must lower your rates or we shall vote those in who will reorganize things. We suggest something in the range of twenty-five to thirty dollars a pop, so that you can at least remain solvent. That is the best alternative. For we still love you. Our desires still burn us from within. Most of us at least skimmed the employee handbook, employees or not, it is an excellent book, so we feel silly when we are yellow. Yet it is as though you exist ouside of us. We are working hard, nonetheless. We work every day to feed the functioning relationship that has developed between us. However, this is proving dysfunctional. We gave you your splendind juniper, but you have let it grow wiley and unkempt. It is all input from our end, with no output from yours. We feed you simply to keep on feeding you. Our needs no longer coalesce. You exist to weave your tapestries, derived from your own hair. We are afraid that we only live under the context of your self-sustainence. We thus demand answers. This is another desire of ours. When will something happen. What will you do next? How shall we handle your inert cyclicality? What have we created?

The actress playing the ebony haired lady twisted in her seat. She looked over her shoulder and called for her manager. He wasn't there, apparently. One of the agrarians attempted to soothe us and ease our fury by explaining that their manager had been going through some things. He was out for the afternoon getting information on the various religions he could join. As it happened, a Wells Fargo courier arrived for me at the gate with a parcel, while the agrarian spoke. The courier's pony neighed and bucked before galloping away. I could not re-sheath my member soon enough to thank him, as indeed, the letter turned out to be a very convenient plot point for Bruno and me. The conflict that tangled itself around us—this insipid research process and our desire to escape it—was settled; how to continue on, there was no more choice to be made. "You're in," the letter informed me. The IRS had approved my application: I was now a fully-registered 501(c)(3) and thus a much more palatable option for future employers, as all subsequent payments to me could be written off as charitable giving. I messaged Dear Reader Human Resources and informed them that, as I was no longer the corporation whose signature they had obtained, the contract we had agreed on was null and void, and that effective immediately neither Bruno nor I were contractually obligated to serve Dear Reader. Yes, the needs of Dear Reader could no longer be conflated with our own. We went back home to Cleveland to find some other gig.

DOCTOR ON A HILL

The doctor, in spite of his troubles, was certain he did his job well. Sometimes bad things happened. He sloughed along the sidewalk, which wrapped around the hill, toward the bus stop, as the hospital administrator had instructed him to. He hung his head and watched the rivulets of springtime melt trickle between his steps.

The hospital for sick and dying children was back there, behind him, at the top of the hill.

Of course children died, he thought. It was no one's fault, generally. It's just a brutal fact of life. Some of them are born with hearts that simply don't work. Despite great strides in medical technology, and despite parents whose jobs provide them with top-of-the-line insurance packages, and, worst, despite the expertise some doctors possess of the human circulatory system, some children die. Some boys, some girls.

So the doctor hung his head. Things appeared on the hill that had before been buried by the snow. A pair of reading glasses appeared in a pile of soggy leaves. The carcass of a squirrel lay on a sewer drain, acted upon by the streaming rivulets. These trickling rivulets resembled the complex reticulation of the human circulatory system. They branched and branched. They also resembled the limbs of the trees dotting the hill around him. The woods concealed the hospital. The trees were rooted in the hill's great steep slopes.

He still wore his white doctor's coat and his headlamp and his stethoscope. He carried his black satchel. No one could deprive him of these things. He resisted the instructions he'd been given to go home, to never return to the hospital. He stood and counted the rivulets. He counted them to take stock, as if it were he who had made them.

"Thirteen, fourteen, fifteen, sixteen . . ." he said.

He ceased counting and thought.

"I am better than they take me for," he said.

He decided to count more things, to appreciate the objects around him. He counted the branches of the trees.

"Eight thousand two hundred seventy-three, eight thousand two hundred seventy-four . . ." he said. The doctor would only stop counting the branches when a car stopped, and its driver asked, "Are you okay?"

The cars lined up. Each driver poked his head out and asked the doctor the same question.

"Are you okay?" they said.

"Everything's fine," the doctor said, "I'm a doctor." The cars peeled away one by one down the side of the hill.

"It's okay," the drivers said. "He's a doctor."

"I save lives. It's what I do. I save lives for a living." He sighed. "Now and then a life is lost rather than saved."

He counted the branches of the trees until the sun receded behind the hill.

"Fifteen thousand and one, fifteen thousand and two . . ."

The top of the hill cast a shadow on the bottom of the hill. The doctor found great mystery in this, that the hill could cast a shadow on top of itself. The shadow grew with each new branch the doctor counted. The shadow effaced the rivulets; it effaced the dwindling snow piles. It was approximately dinner time; he'd be eating if he had chosen to go home.

He turned on his headlamp to give himself light. The growing darkness was greater than the darkness of the hill's shadow on top of itself. He felt his heart beat inside his chest. He listened to it through his stethoscope.

"Torts are civil wrongs recognized by law as grounds for a lawsuit. These wrongs result in an injury or harm constituting the basis for a claim by the injured party. While some torts are also crimes punishable with imprisonment, the primary aim of tort law is to provide relief for the damages incurred and deter others from committing the same harms. The injured person may sue for an injunction to prevent the continuation of the tortious conduct or for monetary damages," his heart said.

The doctor crumpled to the sidewalk and scraped his knee. The blood oozed in accordance with his pulse. He felt his wrist. The pulse in his wrist went, "thump-thump." His slacks and white coat were wet with runoff from the snow. He splashed in the rivulets, which grew and grew. The rivulets raged. He fought the raging rivulets and uncrumpled his crumpled body. He feared the rivulets would pull him to the sewer grate and act upon him there. He dragged his body against the raging rivulets until his body was free of them. He braced himself against the trunk of a tree rooted in the great steep hillside. He turned his stethoscope onto himself once more. He pressed his stethoscope against his own chest, against his wet white coat.

His heart said, "One of the biggest concerns with mandated benefits is that they increase the cost of health care coverage. Some recent examples of mandated benefits include coverage for diabetic supplies, equipment and education, prostate screening antigen (PSA) testing for prostate cancer, bone densitometry for osteoporosis, breast reconstructive surgery following a mastectomy, and mastectomy length-of-stay requirements. We are opposed to the government determining specific benefits to be included in managed care and insurance contracts. We believe that the marketplace should determine the benefits available to health plan participants."

He would have died from shock had he not known about the human circulatory system. He reached for his satchel. He stripped himself from the waist up. He fastened the sticky sensors of the travel defibrilator to his barrel chest, which he zapped. He pressed his stethoscope against himself, listened for his heart, and heard the soft slow breathing of his heart inside his naked barrel chest. The heart snoozed. He could hear it snoring. The doctor's uncrumpled body lay hidden in the darkness of night, against the trunk of the tree rooted in the hillside, wet with water runoff in rivulets from the melting snow. He sighed. His naked barrel chest distended with each deep breath.

The doctor's body would not move in the morning. He looked out at the road, which was jammed with gurneys. He blinked, and the gurneys were cars. The doctor's body was nestled in a pile of leaves. Beside him was a dwindling pile of snow still left from winter.

"I'm alive," he said.

The line of cars traveling to the hospital atop the hill thickened. Their drivers wailed. Their cars resembled gurneys. They moved on wheels and carried patients. The doctor felt okay about this comparison. They looked like gurneys to him.

He noticed the top of a head in the dwindling snow beside him. He felt his heart stir. He studied the top of the head. The scalp was bald with a horseshoe of black hair. There were blemishes from the sun. Slowly the top of its ears emerged. The pulse in his wrist went "thump-thump." He listened to his heart with his stethoscope.

"Co-pay," it said, again and again. "Co-pay. Co-pay. Co-pay."

The doctor wiped the thick wet snow from the head. The snow was black and dirtied with sticks and leaves.

The face was handsome. The eyes were blue and the jaw was strong. The cheeks were clean-shaven. The doctor observed a cleft in the chin. The face's voice was a pleasant and reassuring baritone.

"Welcome to the Newlywed Game," the face said. "We've got some young ones, we've got some old ones. I'll tell you one thing about all four of our couples: they're newlyweds. They've been married less than two years. We'll meet them and ask some questions, right after these words. Alright? Stay with us."

The doctor's heart said, "Co-pay. Co-pay."

The doctor, an expert on the human circulatory system, could not explain to himself why his legs would not move. He wished to lift himself from the pile of leaves and button up his shirt, to sprint to the bottom of the hill, to be swallowed by the hill's shadow of itself.

Some children who came to him liked Star Trek. The child whose life he could not save had liked Star Trek. Instead of candy and ice cream and cards from her classmates, this child asked for toy replicas of the Enterprise, and figurines of Kirk, Spock, Sulu, Uhura, and Bones. She called the doctor Bones.

"Damn it, " he had said, to the child's parents, who held out hope, "I'm a doctor, not a miracle worker."

The face spoke again, "Okay. With the wives secluded safely offstage it's time to start with some five-point questions. Now as you know, gentlemen, you'll be answering these questions as you predict your wife will answer the same question when she returns. If her answer should happen to match your prediction, then you get five points."

"Damn it, I'm a doctor, not God. What are you?"

"And if you have more points than everyone else at the end of the game, you win a grand prize that's been selected especially for you."

"Jesus," the doctor said.

Several weeks later, when the hill's shadow of itself grew and stayed longer, and the piles of snow turned to puddles of slush, the head became a body. The doctor and the body ate mud and leaves for sustenance. No one identified him as a doctor. His coat was off and he was covered in grime. His chest was no longer barrel-like. The body with the talking head was fully suited. It held its arm around the doctor and spoke into a microphone. The microphone was long and skinny. It resembled a child's femur. It was disconnected.

"Who are you possibly speaking for?" the doctor said.

"Gentlemen," the body said, "while you were dating, did your wife say she held back so long it drove you crazy, or gave in so soon you got bored?"

The branches had sprouted buds, which were turning into leaves. The leaves were too innumerable to count. The doctor could not take stock of the leaves. From the line of automobiles, a truck with a flashing yellow siren pulled up to the sidewalk. Two men in luminescent vests climbed out. The melting snow had revealed many carcasses. The men removed the squirrel carcass from the sewer grate with a long metal grabber. The back of the truck was filled with carcasses. Raccoon carcasses. Deer carcasses. Dog carcasses.

The doctor buried his face in the pile of leaves. Perhaps it was his will that his legs should not work. Perhaps his psychiatrist colleagues were onto something. Perhaps he wished misfortune upon himself. He listened to his heart. "Medical malpractice occurs when a hospital, doctor or other health care professional, through a negligent act or omission, causes an injury to a patient. The negligence might be the result of errors in diagnosis, treatment, aftercare or health management," it said.

The doctor groaned. He leaned against the body and hugged it. Though the morning was bright, the doctor turned on his headlamp. Maybe, he thought, it would provide clarity.

He held his stethoscope to his chest. His heart spoke with the voice of the hospital administrator: "It's like this. You have door number one, and you have door number two. Door number one means you leave and we speak well of you. Door number two means you leave because we made you leave. Door number three? That's not even an option. Litigation is never an option in a situation like this. One or two. Which one do you want? Or shall I choose for you?"

"Damn it," the doctor said, "I'm a doctor, not God."

He looked into the body's eyes.

"Make me like you," he said. "Please. Make me like you."

The body held him closer. "Gentlemen," it said, "how did your wife complete this sentence? This is your wife talking. She said, 'When it comes to sex, my husband usually pretends he's what?'"

"For God's sake, make me like you."

The doctor felt around the steep hillside. He found a rock with a flat edge. He slumped forward and struck the flat edge to the sidewalk. He struck the flat edge until it was sharp. He took the sharp edge and ran it through his hair. He ran it through his hair until his hair came off in clumps. He nicked his scalp. The body wiped away the small trickle of blood.

"I'm making myself like you, see?" the doctor said. "I'm a handsome bald man, just like you. I can do Let's Make a Deal. I can sit here and talk to no one. I can ask which it will be, door number one or door number two. The brand new car or the pack mule." He ran the sharpened rock through his hair. He spoke into his stethoscope like it was a microphone. The days passed and the trees came into bloom. The shadow cast by the hill was effaced by the shadows cast by the trees. The sun came through and mottled the doctor's head with bright spots. Over and over again he said, "Door one, door two? Door one, door two

. . ." He and the body spoke. Their voices reached no one. The line of cars continued into autumn. Soon there were flurries. The flurries began to accumulate.

CADILLAC MAN

The swatch of dirt had not always been in the family. It was Indian land once, and before that, as Conrad Brady always says, it belonged only to the wildlife and the sacred maker. It was harnessed, subdued, and made tenable by the first who roamed it, then rediscovered and stolen and turned into something else entirely—a pioneer outpost, a dumping ground, an incinerator, a lot deemed vacant by the laws of private property—and now, under the Brady name a full century after the family obtained it, it's a scrap heap, tucked behind a Ford dealership and the Super Walmart.

The thruway skirts the edge of this diverse sector. The traffic to the west seems to underline old Conrad's voice when he says this kind of stuff about the frailty of their ownership, the blind luck that allows them to call this place theirs. The hum of various motor vehicles does not intrude upon him. Nor does it make his voice seem small. Not when he talks to his boy, Clint. Nor when he is alone, reminiscing about what he has.

This morning as he drives, Conrad Brady, in hushed murmurs, points out to no one but himself that despite their family's particular history on this parcel, the scrap yard which they have built on it belongs to them.

Every last inch.

He'll tell it this way to the journalist from Sioux Falls who is coming to visit this afternoon, mainly, Conrad supposes, to ask about the family's other luck, the scratch-off ticket that made Conrad an even wealthier man, which hangs framed in the office he shares with the boy. But Conrad, a man of strong resolve, knows he won't lose focus. He'll tell this journalist how, on its centennial birthday, the other folks in Mankato still refer to the scrap yard by the Bradys' name, as in: I got a old washer I need taken to Brady's. When are you bringing that Yugo to Brady's—I got some shit I need to get rid of. Them Bradys are the people of junk and the scrap handling magnet.

And how by this—Brady—they mean the patch of earth.

They have meant it this way for decades.

Indian Jim makes footprints in the dirt and counts scrap, pile by pile.

He numbers the crushed washing machines.

He arranges the disembodied fenders in rows of two.

He gives names to the bundle of TV antennas tangled in the lot's corner, where the fence has been peeled back from its post by some anonymous being. Coyote, perhaps, or Spider. Some human thief.

This antenna is Wasp Removed From Nest. That one, Glistening Snake. And on top, Antler Without a Head.

None of this belongs to him.

He records his count on the receipts that Clint, the boy, the miserable boy as tall and cumbersome as a sasquatch, gave him, to make sure nothing has gone missing. The receipts are clipped to a board and composed of three sheets each: a white one on top, then a yellow, then a pink, of which the latter two record his writings in faded imprints. His scrawls are messy. The blue pen is tiny between his wracked and swollen hands. He has turned many wrenches, dug many holes, broken the teeth of many drunkards in his time. He is tall, though not as tall as the boy; the heaps go just twice as high as Indian Jim stands. The old man calls them crags, or gorges, or mountains. The old man calls them extensions of the soil. The old man calls him Tonto or Sue, the lady's name, in moments of anger and heightened intensity, or simply to make fun. The old man brags about the Brady home, which he has named "Sod House." It rests in the wedge of dirt where the river bends north like a crimped, useless pipe. The old man calls the river the Tigris and Euphrates. The old man does not understand that of which he speaks. The old man does not understand much.

Katie Gardner departs downtown Sioux Falls in the Ford Ranger lent to her by the Argus Ledger. She coasts along the I-90 corridor between towns that have stood for 100 years or less. Between them are short, grassy buttes and plains that flatten as she heads east. Small towns whose economies are surprisingly robust. There's great money in churning earth, in soaking it with confusing blends of fertilizer and poison. Or, like the subject of her afternoon interview has done, covering it with junk.

She passes through Brandon, Luverne, Worthington. At a stoplight in Sherburn, she gets caught behind a brand new six-wheel Chevy that rumbles along like a shiny waxed buffalo. She only notices because it is so common. The driver turns off the main road and there is a different truck in front of her, a gleaming Ford with a heavy steel winch fixed to its rear bumper. In a field outside town, a team of combines cuts acres of yellow wheat as if to erase it from the face of the earth. There are signs posted in the ditch: Freyr by Syngenta.

Conrad pulls in and sees Indian Jim going around, marking receipts tarnished by wrinkles and rings from coffee mugs set on them.

He enters the office and throws down his keys.

"What's Tonto doing out there? Why ain't he on the scale?"

"I got him on a top to bottom count," Clint says. "Had a hole in the fence this morning where someone could've snuck in."

"You get it fixed?"

"Will later."

"What do you got Billy doing?"

"He's handling the magnet."

"Right now?"

"Yup."

"Just sitting in there?"

"Yup."

"Well what the fuck is there for him to move?" Conrad says. "Dipshit." He hobbles to the far wall and pours himself coffee. "Any other news? If not I think I'll wash up for my big interview." He loosens the strings of his bolo tie. The denim underside of his breast is already blotted with sweat, wet spotty arches strung like an archipelago, broken fragments dotting his torso.

"A man from Saint Peter called yesterday evening," Clint says. "Left us a message. He says he's got a Cadillac he wants to get rid of. Says it's like new. You want me to call him back?"

"What's he want to get rid of a new Cadillac for?" Conrad says.

"Don't know," Clint says, shrugging. His chair doesn't have armrests. He wouldn't fit if it did. "Hey, maybe depending on how nice it is, you could take the Caddy for yourself and I could have your truck? We'd each have a ride, then."

"Hell no," Conrad says. "You think this is a damn trading post? Is your skull that thick?" He unbuttons his shirt. "Go ahead," he says. "Give him a call." He picks up a handkerchief from the desk and wets it in the bathroom sink. He wipes his hands and chest, then his face. He reaches for the sack of Red Man in his back pocket and pinches a giant brown wad between his fingers and folds it inside his cheek. He dumps his coffee, which is from yesterday. He spits into the cup.

No one can guess how old Indian Jim is. When they ask about his tattoos, his answers surprise them.

The one on his shoulder is a face—Buffalo Bill's, the old west gun show exhibitor, with his eyes X-ed out.

The wings of Thunderbird span the width of his back, lightning bolts shooting from its eyes.

On his forearm is the eagle perched atop the anchored globe from his days tromping jungle bush between Saigon and Hanoi. On the other forearm, etched after his discharge from the Marines, the encircled profile of a plains warrior, head dressed in a hand flashing hippie peace against a striped plane of black, yellow, white, and red: the logo of his A.I.M. brothers, who stood beside him at the second Wounded Knee.

"You were an adult back then?" people sometimes say.

"Yes."

"You don't look old enough. How long have you been around?"

"As long as I have been."

"How tall are you?"

"This tall."

"Are you as tall as Conrad's boy? What's his name?"

"No."

"What's that bird on your back?"

"Wakinyan."

"What's that mean?"

He stands before a pyramid of wooden TV sets with their screens smashed. There is an axle, too, and several aluminum ladders laid flat, rungs missing or sprung like broken guitar strings. He marks these items down. His jeans are caked in yellow dust. His black hair seals in heat. He used to have a TV like one of these. He's never had cable or a telephone or an internet connection. He watched networks on the antenna when he owned a TV. He hasn't seen a TV like this since he can remember. He reads his news in the paper each day. He turns to see if the old man or the boy are watching him from behind. There's no one left for him to go home to.

Katie Gardner arrives a little after ten o'clock. She parks the newspaper's pickup beside a brand new Silverado, pearly white, which must belong to the proprietor. The parking lot is gravel and is littered with potholes. There is a white sign on the fence with plain red lettering: Brady Iron and Scrap. She wonders how much money a scrap yard takes in annually, or in a single day, or the extent to which the lottery has affected Conrad Brady's life.

A group of men huddles beneath a shingled overhang near the gate. A potbellied dude, perhaps a local, in a plaid snap shirt and seed cap. Complexion specked with dirt. Beside him, a very tall man, towheaded, dressed in denim. The tall man's jeans are tucked into his boots. They each lean on different sides of a car, a Cadillac. It looks almost brand new. Another spoil of the state lottery, perhaps. An older fellow—the proprietor, certainly—steps out of the office and shouts at the towhead, "Got off her, you oaf. You'll fuck up her glimmer."

The towhead backs away and stands tall, tightening his fists, two globes hanging at his waist.

"What're you gonna do?" the old man says.

A Native approaches them and sets a clipboarded wad of papers on the ground, securing them with a stone.

Katie surveys the establishment. The scrap heaps loom. They cast shadows across the dirt. She joins the huddle. No one seems to notice.

The Native hops in the Cadillac and steers it onto the scale, a large steel platform with iron bumpers running along each side. Conrad Brady totters in small circles as the scale spits out the vehicle's weight on a slip of paper. He wheezes between mirthful chuckles, turning to Katie, thrusting a thumb back over his shoulder. He flicks his eyebrows up and down, perhaps to indicate his satisfaction with the great American automobile being taken in before them.

"It's ours now," the towhead grumbles. He crosses his arms. "Sure as shit."

They all watch as the Native pulls the Cadillac forward off the scale and parks it in the clearing where it will be elevated and moved. He gets out, lights a cigarette, and stands by himself near the end of the lot. A frumpy teenager works across the way in the cab of the scrap magnet. Maybe 17 or 18 years old, already quite obese. There's some kind of logo on his shirt. Hunting or racing. It's obscured by the dirty glass of the magnet's cab. The boy wears a camouflage cap, the brim of which is curved almost into a complete circle. His hair sticks out around his ears like dry grass.

The machine's heavy arm swings directly above the Cadillac. The boy turns on the magnet, and various screws and spikes and other twisted bits get sucked up out of the dirt like a spill in reverse. The Cadillac doesn't budge until the magnet warms up some. When this happens the vehicle trembles, and its wheels begin to lift and drop. The Cadillac looks like it's making a true effort to resist the force acting upon it from above, until soon it relents and it too gets lifted. There is a deep mechanical groan as the boy swings it to the side of the scrap yard and places it atop a mound of crushed objects, some of which appear to have been vehicles once, as well. Flattened headlights. Steel bumpers twisted and elongated like warm taffy.

Conrad spits.

"You're the journalist, I suppose," he shouts above the deep wail of the machine.

"That's right," she says. "You must be Conrad."

"In the flesh."

He grabs her shoulder and starts in on pride and history and whatnot as he points at the slow swinging Cadillac.

"It'll be crushed this afternoon, which is the thing," he shouts. "We ain't special because this place is fit for a Caddy. We're special because we can take a perfectly good one and crush it to smithereens, no questions asked. Been doing it this way for a hundred years."

She doesn't say anything.

"That motherfucker," Conrad muses, "on top that mountain of shit, is pristine. Not sure why in the hell this yokel wants to get rid of her."

No one, including Katie, can deny the object's beauty, how it suppresses the many facets of its design. The blue paint, reminiscent of the sky's infinite archways, is a firmament in miniature. The car's old owner collects his check from the towhead and leaves. She watches the Native smoke, his back against the brick office. Conrad pulls Katie closer and says he would drive the thing home himself if it wasn't proper to turn the son of a bitch into a lustrous 2,500 pound brick.

Indian Jim is a highly skilled marksman. When he was a boy, his family lived in a one-room structure in the woods near the river with a potbelly stove and a single skinny window. He shared a mattress with his seven siblings and hunted chipmunks during the day with stones and a leather thong. He was the second-oldest child. His father would sit outside their home on a stump all day drinking corn alcohol distilled by other unemployed Indians. His mother died in the birth of the youngest child. Jim's father would tell his children that the government gave Indians alcohol to ruin their bodies and break their collective spirit. An Indian couldn't stand up for himself if he was too drunk to balance. He said it was a great perversion that they depended on the U.S. government for income. He drank every single day. He drank so much that as an old man he was blind. Their tiny house was located on the edge of a grass field. The neighbors were all Indians and lived within sight. It was a mile or so outside of town. They called it the Rez even though it wasn't a reservation. Sioux weren't allowed to have one of those in Minnesota. The grass was always high and swayed in the wind. Jim's oldest brother, Norman, would shovel snow in the winter with pieces of bark he'd collected the previous spring. They had no phone lines or electricity or running water.

One day, when Jim was thirteen, a man from the police station came to the Rez to tell the children about law enforcement. This policeman said that he was $1/16^{th}$ Chippewa. He explained how policemen were friends, and that if their dads ever drank too much and became violent, they should call the police for help. He brought two rifles with him, a .30-06 and a .22. He asked the kids how many of their dads kept guns in the house. Jim and Norman and the dozen or so other children raised their hands. The policeman shook his head and expressed his regret that their fathers found the resources for alcohol and weaponry but couldn't manage to feed their own kids or give them all shoes. Later, the police officer set up a pyramid of tin cans and let the older boys shoot at them. Norman handled the .22 and hit two cans. Thomas Jefferson Dirty Belly, a year younger than Norman and a year older than Jim, used the other rifle and missed the cans completely. Jim used the same rifle and plunked each can, the one on top, then the row of two in the middle, and finally the row of three on the dirt. He did not miss once. The policeman patted his head and gave him a toy badge. He told Jim there might be a future for him in law enforcement if he didn't turn into a drunk who sat on a stump all day.

Jim did not become a police officer. He used his skills

to shoot communists in Vietnam. He used them to blow out the knee of a federal marshal in South Dakota, after which he hid in the woods for six days hunting chipmunks with rocks. He doesn't fire guns anymore. He lives in an efficiency apartment in the old German end of town. He has never once in his life imbibed.

The Cadillac pitches now in the wind. Its shadow grows long and short. Old Conrad doesn't fret. The thing is heavy. He sits back in his chair and listens to the classifieds on the radio. His concern, he tells the journalist, is with the various asking prices for unwanted items, particularly those which are metallic and heavy. The day's paper is spread across his lap. Several unladen trucks are lined up outside. Their drivers are anxious to leave. There is a stack of checks on the desk waiting to be signed.

"Why does the price matter?" the journalist says, referring to the classifieds. "Can't you just use your lottery money?"

"My lotto cash? Shit. What kind of a way is that to run a business?" He leans over and spits a little brown bomb into the Folger's can beside his desk. "That's all for personal financing. My house and the like. My truck. I won't invest it in the business, except what I need to keep it going. Hell no." He dabs his forehead with the handkerchief. The boy comes out of the bathroom wiping his hands on his shirt. "Plus," Conrad says, "I gotta make sure this bonehead has something to live on after I kick the bucket. He's been here his whole life, yet he don't know a work order from his ass cheek."

Clint stops and lengthens his spine. His face melts into a profound scowl. "I know what a work order is," he says. "That's them, right there." He points to a stack of papers on the filing cabinet beside the door.

"Looky here," Conrad says. "You must be Adam, naming the shit he sees."

The boy's skin turns red as he runs a hand through his hair. He leans forward and pounds his fist on the old man's desk. He breaths deeply. His chest and shoulders heave. His eyes are streaked with rage.

Conrad leans back in his chair and looks at Katie. "See what I have to live with?" he says. "Temper tantrum after temper tantrum."

The journalist sets down her pen and scratches her neck. The boy's face scrunches. He begins to cry. "I gotta go fix the god damn fence," he whimpers. He wipes his nose with his sleeve. His forearm is slicked with snot and drool. He grabs a rubber mallet from the old man's desk and tromps outside, leaving the door open behind him.

"Moron," Conrad says. "Can't shut the door when the AC is on."

Katie Gardner clears her throat. Her skin has reddened, too. "So," she says, "you were saying you keep your lottery winnings separate from your business finances."

"God damn. Is that all you want to ask about is my lotto winnings? The Free Press already did a story about it. Why don't you go dig that story up if it interests you so much?" He spits again. The journalist, hardly out of childhood it seems, with her flouncing hair and glistening eyes and rosy cheeks like the pictures of the Virgin hanging in church, recoils at the sound of the little splash.

"No sir," she says. "That's not all I'm interested in. Not by any means."

"Well shoot, then. Let me have it."

Katie Gardner, a field reporter in the fourth year of her career at the Argus Ledger, is in deep in the process of writing and publishing one of the most extensive recent series on the current state of Dakota tribal members. Her project is centered on the Pine Ridge Reservation, which serves as exemplar of the poverty and depletion of contemporary tribal life. In the previous year or so, she has filled three dozen notebooks with interview transcripts given to her by elders, men, women, and children, detailing their days spent studying the language, working as nurses, going to school, sitting around and drinking, eating cheese and peanut butter dispensed by government agencies, smoking cigarettes, looking at the sky, listening to the wind, watching ballgames on TV, drawing shapes in the dirt, tidying their houses. Katie has never been poor herself. She grew up in Sisseton and went to the state college in Brookings and got a job in Sioux Falls straight out of school. She feels confident that her student loans will be paid in full by the time she's 32. She visits her parents sometimes on the weekends and on all major holidays. She drives a Prius with 36,000 miles on the odometer.

She can explain neither to herself nor to Conrad Brady her interest in taking on such a project. Sometimes, when she's driving home in the early night from some assignment about a local sculptor or the opening of a new grocery store, she imagines that the cars transform into buffaloes, the streets into plains of swaying switchgrass. Sometimes there's someone out walking—an old lady becomes a scout or a fearful deserter. Her high school soccer coach was gung-ho about spirit and the curation of school traditions. "You didn't plant this field," he would say. "You didn't dig the well that gives you water." She removes these sayings from their context and chews on them the way Brady chews his Red Man. She finds herself frequently wondering if a person died on the place she stands, or if some holy ritual was performed there, or nothing so important, if she simply shares footsteps with a man or woman or child who roamed here centuries earlier.

The project feels like the indulgence of her natural sense of wonder, she tells the proprietor. That being so near the site of the largest public execution in United States history—the 1862 hanging of thirty-eight Dakota after the infamous land grab and subsequent uprising—it only made sense to trace the origins of Pine Ridge. She'd already been to Saint Peter, Fort Ridgely, and New Ulm. She'd already visited the site of the execution, now called Reconciliation Park, beside Mankato's civic center. She'd already dug through archives, found the names of those tried, those pardoned, and those executed; those in charge, those on the peripheries, those whose names were included in some log for no other reason than miserable happenstance.

"I'm interested," she says, "in the things we know about ourselves that we simply refuse to see. The stuff that gets lost through history and churns up in places we don't expect to find them."

"Well," the old man says, "if you feel so damn guilty about things that happened a hundred doggone years ago, we got ourselves a Sioux right outside. Maybe he can make you a head dress to wear around if you say pretty please." He hooks his finger and fishes the plug of tobacco from his cheek and drops it in the can. He stands and retreats into the bathroom. He closes the door behind him.

Clint is now thirty-four years old and six-feet, ten-inches tall, a whole foot greater than his father. He is in the tall grass with a rubber mallet, banging the fence back into shape. He mutters about thieves, about the right he has to keep what's in the family. There is a space large enough for a man to fit his body through, but it is not big enough for Clint. The clanging echos of his mallet blend with the air rippling over the interstate. His hand swallows the handle. His straining skin is flecked with red. The shirt on his back strains at the seams. His knees creak and join his spine in a sorrowful chorus of pops. When he stands, his skeleton screams.

There is no breeze today, again. The whole summer has been windless. One long day in which the leaves and grass have not once flicked. The sun is very hot. The smell of the drainage ditch near the scrap yard lifts and percolates the afternoon. Clint can tell that the dank scent will be thick all evening like an impassable fog. Many suns aim their rays directly at his squint. He sweeps a glistening forearm across his glistening brow. His skin, like a pig's, glistens. All his inches glisten. He is surrounded by slop. His slop. His father's slop. His family's slop, there for him to roll around in. Somehow it has value. He has a stake in this buildup of junk, whether his father will say so or not.

Billy Morgan, a part-timer, strolls out of the scrap yard and winks at Clint. He gets in his Escort and drives away. It's just Clint left who can operate the magnet if need be, although he hates doing it because the cab is cramped and he has to leave the door open and let his legs hang out when he's running it, which is dangerous. He enters the lot to make sure the Indian isn't sitting down, maybe drawing circles or stick figures in the dirt, his legs crossed, long pipe exuding smoke, or banging some skin drum to bring rain. The Indian stares at a pile. Clint sees the Cadillac resting atop a mound of shit. Its shadow is long and bent and reminds him of a depressed person. He passes the Indian with steps he makes heavy. All his life he's been among these heaps of scrap, kept here as if he himself was a spare part. The Indian should count him, should feel his presence.

The notion arises within his gut to climb the mound. He braces his feet between the crushed bodies and heaves himself upward. He reaches the minor summit in two strides and rests his shoulder against the car. It's heavy. He touches its steel body and then his own body, much softer and full of nerves.

Across the way, the reporter walks to her truck and leaves.

He is not a spare part. He is not a fender or a hubcap or an empty trunk. God damn this place, he thinks, and all the shit kept within its walls, piling up year after year as if the moments themselves gather here. He leans harder against the vehicle, rocks back, and thrusts his body into the passenger door. God damn his father's profits. The Cadillac doesn't tumble immediately. He sweats through his blue shirt, leans back, and thrusts himself again. He screams. The car moans, softly and then louder, as the dual forces of gravity and Clint's weight act upon it and it pitches further forward and is overtaken by its own weight, rolling over like a dead man.

Indian Jim punches his card. On it, the hours that have accrued are stamped. He leaves the inventory sheets in their clipboard and places them in a slot by the office door. He thinks about the Cadillac as he gets in his Jeep Cherokee and turns the engine over, the same late 80s model he has been driving since the early 2000s. The old man, whenever he sees Jim pull in, asks how the vehicle's Injun is running. The old man has locked himself away. The old man lingers here for long hours. The old man seems to always be home, whether at the scrap yard or Sod House, or anyplace else. The old man stakes a claim on this world.

Indian Jim's vehicle gets eleven miles per gallon. The engine burns a quart of oil every month. He drives along the main drag, past the Olive Garden, the Home Goods, and the city's mall. The radio is turned to the local news. There is a story about a group of families who lost their homes in the recession and lived in tents they pitched in a wooded area a mile or so south of town. They stayed there for nearly a year. The reporter is amazed that such a lifestyle could be maintained for more than a few days. This is followed by a weather report. More heat. More sun. Soon Jim sees a tall denim figure walking along the shoulder of the road. He slows to pick up the boy, but is honked at by the truck behind him as the boy waves him along.

Indian Jim has three cans of chicken noodle soup

and half a jar of peanut butter in the cabinet at home. He counted over 2500 parts today to make sure none had left the Bradys' lot. All the pieces were there, each one accounted for, and it was as if his numbering of things had reinvented the place, renewing the existence of that small world the old man holds sacred. The stoplight ahead burns red and he stops, shuts off the radio. The old man needs a name. Sleeping Bear. Wobbling Horse. Cadillac Man.

PHYSICALLY ALARMING MEN

After the dog died in January, Bob's typical mopiness turned to nostalgia for his childhood house. It had been a long winter with a lot of cold and not much snow. Janice spent her afternoons drinking instant jasmine tea. On most nights she'd add several fingers of brandy. She did crossword puzzles and watched TV shows about life in America's toughest prisons. Every Monday, she also watched two hours of professional wrestling, cowering beneath the afghan each time an elbow crashed into someone's skull.

The ground was too frozen to dig a grave for the dog. Bob wrapped the thing in a tarp and stored it behind the tool shed until the dirt was soft enough for him to stick a shovel into it. His plan was to bury the dog under Janice's hyacinths. She didn't talk to him for a week after he suggested his idea. Twice, she woke in the middle of the night clawing at his shoulders. When April came, Bob changed his mind and suggested burying the dog in the backyard of his childhood house, next to the collie his family had owned forty years earlier, on the other side of the state.

"Where I grew up," he said, tightening something under the sink, "everyone knew everyone. There wasn't a stranger around, and if there was, we took him in and made him feel at home."

When the thaw came, halfway through May, Bob loaded the dog's body into a forty-quart cooler. He packed it in the back seat along with Janice's gardening tools, which were wrapped in brown canvas and tied with a piece of twine. She hardly noticed the annoying tune he hummed, because Bob was always humming to himself. Instead she chose to feel amazement at the frost boil she stood on. If she put her foot on its center, the ground swelled around the edges. When she raised her foot, the ground flattened. She imagined a great blackness beneath her, cavernous acres filled with the skeletons of household pets.

"Why don't we bury him here?" she said. "Under this frost boil? It would save us a trip."

"Are you crazy? What if the ground gives and his body spills out? How horrifying would that be?"

They headed east on the two lane highway. Janice flipped through a book. She didn't retain a single word. The book was a murder mystery. Someone had died, and no one knew who killed her.

They pulled into a reservation town after an hour and a half.

"I need a milkshake," Bob said. His long fingernails were grimy from peeling the dog's carcass off the ground. He wore his only suit and the fedora with the yellow feather tucked in the band. His job as a roving burglar alarm salesman had conditioned him to dress elegantly when traveling, but his elegance had limits; the jacket was much too big and made him seem like a cheapskate. Janice wore a white sweater she had discovered in the back of her closet three weeks earlier, behind the plastic bag containing her wedding dress. She didn't know how old it was. She didn't remember even buying it. It fit her perfectly.

They found a diner on the edge of a lake. Bob went inside for his snack. The lake was silver and still and frozen around the edges. It had melted from the inside out. Janice walked down to the rocky shore and listened to the surface of the water break apart and mend itself. She had collected rocks when she was a girl. She remembered placing them in a little motorized bin that would spin them around and around. She'd line the polished bits of granite and shale along her bedroom windowsill and marvel at the gleaming forms. She couldn't remember the last time she'd held a polished rock, where it was, or when, or on what occasion. She picked a flat one off the shore and chucked it sidearm at the water. It skipped once and sank. Bob came out of the diner an hour later and called her name. She climbed back to the parking lot and saw him scraping his incisors with a toothpick, the sports section tucked under his arm.

"Nothing good happens in a place like this," he announced.

Immediately outside of the town, there were people walking on the shoulder of the highway. At least a dozen of them. Their long black hair was tied in braids. They wore t-shirts and shorts and marched single-file carrying armloads of woven welcome mats. Behind them was a single set of footprints they all shared. Janice's mother had owned a photograph of similar footprints, only they were barefoot and on a piece of shoreline. A Bible verse was printed in the bottom corner of the photograph. She didn't remember how the verse went, or from which book it was excerpted. They passed the marchers, who didn't look sad, like Janice expected.

"Those idiots must be freezing!" Bob said. "Did you know that when these people turn eighteen, the government cuts every single one of them a big fat royalty check, just for being alive? That's why they live in trailers and drive brand new pickups, even though they're a bunch of piss poor drunks." He rolled down his window to yell at them.

"Slow down. You'll hit somebody."

"I will not."

Janice spotted a yellow barn on the side of the road. An old station wagon pulled out from a gravel lot in front of it and drove so slowly Bob hit the brakes and nearly went into a skid.

"Animals!" he said.

Janice threw the murder mystery at his head and knocked his fedora out the window.

"What in the hell was that for?" he said. He gaped at the receding grayness in the driver's side mirror and then at Janice. "That's just perfect!"

He pulled into the gravel lot in front of the barn and muttered to himself as he walked toward the highway. He was so worked up he began to cough. Janice stared at his inordinate shoulders as he walked right through the marchers and disturbed their perfect line.

It turned out the big yellow barn housed the county flea market. Inside, six buzzing lights hung from the ceiling and swayed slightly in the cross draft. Small green weeds sprouted from the cement floor, rooted there like good and loyal sons. A person could purchase many different things in this place. There were dishes, picture frames, homemade soaps, nursery furniture, and weapons of all sorts—knives, throwing stars, machetes, walking sticks that converted into long skinny shivs if you unscrewed the handles.

Janice shuffled among a rack of t-shirts with professional wrestlers on them. The wrestlers looked angry and flexed their oily upper bodies. She couldn't understand their elaborate costumes. One had pink streamers in his hair. His face was painted like a dog's. Another was bald and had no front teeth. A third was dressed in a long black coat with the brim of his hat pulled low, covering his eyes. They were accompanied by slogans as terrifying as their scowls: "Who's Next?"; "Here Comes the Pain!"; "Rest in Peace."

The highway marchers stopped at a table and dropped their welcome mats on it. One of them pulled a cash box from a plastic bucket under the table as the rest dispersed. They all crowded toward a particular corner of the barn, to a long glass case between a saddle stand and a woman selling fried dough from a shopping cart. The case was lit up from the inside. A neon sign buzzed above it: gun show. Janice picked up a saucer and a tea cup. Some old lady had loved this thing and then died.

The gun show clerk had a big ring of keys on his belt that he used to unlock the case. He stuck his pudgy torso inside and came out holding a magnificent assault rifle, the kind Janice had seen so often on the news, whenever a mass murder occurred. A man waiting at the counter grabbed it from him. This customer held the weapon to his shoulder as if to take aim. He was very tall and smiled brightly. His skin was oily and white as fresh snow and stretched shiny over his impressive musculature. He looked very much like he could have been a wrestler on TV. Janice once had a college professor who described everything white as "alabaster." This professor was quite handsome and read Shakespeare out loud in a French accent and threatened to fail anyone who mistook Romeo for a Capulet. For months, Janice had said the word to herself, "alabaster." The pages of her textbooks were alabaster. Her teeth were alabaster. So were the snow drifts on the frozen ground. So were her bones.

She was startled by a hand on her shoulder. Long white fingers. It was Bob's hand. He spun her around. His bald head was splotchy pink and the veins in his temples were throbbing. He grinned and held up his fedora.

"Nice work," he said. The thing was crushed like a used soda can. The feather was missing.

"How do you know they'll let us bury him?" Janice said.

"What? Who?"

"The dog! We have to bury our dog!"

"I know that," Bob said. He gripped the hat with both hands and thrust it atop his head, restoring the shape of the dented crown. "Do you think I don't know that? Jesus. What a stupid thing to say."

Sometimes Janice felt as if the ground beneath her feet would crack in elaborate patterns, and the earth would pull itself apart and let loose all of the things buried throughout history, which would drift away, item by item. She was afraid she'd be left standing on a mere bit of gravel or on some shape she never knew existed, some secret geometry that would spell for her the difference between being and having been. The customer with the gun must have stood nearly seven feet tall. The weapon looked like a bottle opener in his hands. He threw down some cash and walked out in front of them with the thing resting on his shoulder.

"Christ," Bob said. He grabbed her by the wrist and pulled her out of the flea market, past the glass case full of assault rifles. She eyed the weapons and shuffled past according to Bob's pull. He helped her into the car then leaned across her to start the ignition.

"I gotta visit the port-o-john," he said. "Don't move."

Janice watched him disappear behind the corner, and it was as if he had never been around to begin with. Her father, it occurred to her, had been the one to set up the rock polishing machine. She would merely sit with her chin in her hands watching the metal bin spin around and around, marveling at the sounds made by little bits of tumbling earth, while he worked solemnly at the kitchen table in a cone of yellow light loading shotgun shells by hand. She scooted over and put the car into gear and turned onto the highway, unsure of where she was heading.

"How about that?" she said. She looked at the cooler and gardening tools in the mirror. It all bounced when the car bounced. "How about that?"

Five miles down the road a column of black smoke rose from the ditch. Janice pulled over. A pickup truck had gone in nose first. The front was submerged in mud and slush and the rear tires spun as if trying to grip the air. The customer she had seen at the flea market sat on the shoulder of the highway with his knees to his chest and the assault rifle strapped to his back. He stood and took a pull from a silver flask. She rolled down the window and asked if his name was Bob.

"Nope," he said. He jangled when he moved even though Janice couldn't see any chains or stray metal on him. He wore blue jean shorts that stopped halfway down his thighs and a black T-shirt with white lettering: *See You at Rehab*.

"Do you need a ride?" she said.

He took the gun off his back and hugged it to his chest. The gesture made his hands appear gentle despite their immensity. Janice figured he could have gripped her around the waist with a single fist and thrown her into the sun. His shoulders rippled with inborn strength. They were flecked with red spots. He had tied his hair into a long pony tail since leaving the flea market, revealing ears that were pierced with small pieces of bone. Without saying anything, he opened the door and squeezed his body inside the car.

"You're a big guy," Janice said.

"Mmhm."

"I bet you could do a slam dunk."

He grunted. Janice turned toward the town.

"Wrong direction," he said.

"What?"

"Home's that-a-way." He tapped the window with the barrel of his gun. "I believe that you intend to take me home." He rested the gun in his lap and grinned at her with a mouth full of gold teeth.

"Don't you want to get help for your truck?"

"Ain't my truck."

They rode with the radio off. The customer rolled down the window and smoked. His hair caught in the wind and blew in fiery red tatters. He finished his cigarette in three deep drags.

Once, in a house they had long since moved out of, Janice fired Bob's handgun at a burglar. She missed. The burglar stole one silver candlestick and was never caught.

The police asked where Bob was. Janice told them he was away, selling burglar alarms. She couldn't remember which house this occurred in, or when. They had lived in seven separate places since they were married.

The customer looked at her and pinched his lips tight. He asked her questions about her personal life, what she was doing out here driving around alone. She had a difficult time answering. She had never thought much about herself.

"Turn here," he finally said. She turned south on a red road spongy from the thaw. It bubbled up every so often and made steering difficult. He pointed the assault rifle out the window and without warning blasted a string bullets into the ditch. The sun emerged from behind a cloud.

"Good thing about plunking earthworms is they're already buried when they get hit."

"Is that so?" Janice said.

"What's in the cooler?"

"It's nothing."

"Don't smell like nothing."

"Do I turn any time soon?"

"Nope." He rolled up his window and lit another cigarette, though he let this one burn slowly. They drove south for several miles. Janice wasn't sure if they were still on the reservation. They passed a sign that said the county stopped maintaining the road beyond a certain point shortly ahead. The road turned abruptly from grated gravel to large rocks, some as big as grapefruits. The cooler jostled. She and the customer bounced in their seats. He let the assault rifle jump like a heated popcorn seed in his lap. Soon they came along a grassy inlet.

"Turn here."

"It's too muddy," she said. "I'll get stuck."

"Stuck don't matter." He picked up the gun and caressed the barrel. His gold teeth glistened. They were so shiny and pristine Janice wondered if he'd let them churn in a motorized bin. His knees pressed against the dashboard. She worried they'd leave permanent impressions. She drove slowly and held the wheel so tightly that her biceps burned. The customer began to hum a tune, something Janice had never heard from Bob nor herself nor anyone. He pulled the rifle's bolt catch and put his cigarette out on the seat.

"Stop here."

"Here?"

There was nothing around but tall grass and a shadowless tree and a lilac bush. The air had grown cooler and a brown fog appeared as if the spirit of the dirt itself had risen. He got out and stretched his arms with the weapon held high above his head. Janice's sweater began to itch. The area was flat and desolate and, with the exception of a few tree lines several miles off, unobstructed. A scream could echo for miles and nobody would hear it. Janice had initially put on her gardening sneakers before leaving the house, but Bob insisted she wear something with heels.

"After you," the customer said. He pointed the gun at her from his waist.

"Which way?"

He flicked the barrel toward the tree. They slogged through ten yards of mud and grass until the ground swelled and they came upon a wooden bulkhead.

"Don't look," he said, crouching down. "I can feel it if you look or not." The combination lock was embedded in the door, just like the one on the fireproof safe behind Janice's wedding dress, where she kept her diamond ring. A wind rose up and she hugged herself for warmth. The lilac bush was in full bloom.

"Alabaster," she said. "That's what you are."

"The hell does that mean?"

She eyed his skin and the bits of gray bone piercing his ear lobes.

"It means I want to touch your shoulder if you'll let me."

He rose and opened the bulkhead to the clamor of gunshots—strings of bullet fire layered over individual blasts. She picked out the sounds of .270s and .30-06s, the calibers her father used on his deer hunts. She had gone with him several times to bond but always wound up spelling words out of rocks in the clearing around his stand. The customer looked her over.

"I ain't into old broads," he said. He pointed the gun barrel down the dark stairwell and grabbed her wrist with his free hand. "You first."

"Can I bring my dog with me?"

"Your what?"

"My dog. He's what's in the cooler."

"Only if we can use it for a target."

"You're quite imposing." Janice fetched the cooler. "Has anyone ever told you that? How imposing you are?"

"My brothers are more so. Here they come, in fact. Fun guys, if you ask me."

Two men appeared in the bulkhead as if summoned by some ritual, each a whole head taller than the customer. Their chests were strapped with ammo and they each had two rifles fastened to their backs like angel wings.

"Bob would be terrified by this," she said. She looked at the cooler. "Can you believe this?"

The customer instructed her to sit on the cooler, so she did. The men arranged themselves around her, the customer in front, flanked behind by his brothers, shiny alabaster figures with hair down to their waists. The brothers each grabbed a handle and lifted Janice.

"I dig your sweater," the one brother said.

"Where did you get it?" said the other one.

"I don't remember. It horrifies me that you're carrying me. You really freak me out."

The brown fog parted around the bulkhead and the four of them went down. On their way the gunshots rang out and the brothers hummed a tune and Janice marveled at the glowing lilac bush. She wondered who came all the way out here to maintain it and trim it into its unique shape, which she had not seen before; she couldn't name the shape even if these brothers pressed their guns to her head and demanded it. They descended, one step at a time. The sound of gunshots grew into a sustained, complicated blare, and the lilac bush disappeared above the threshold. For a moment everything was black, and in that moment Janice pictured Bob standing alone on the highway with a bundle of welcome mats in his arms, kicking rocks at every car that passed. She wondered what had happened to his plan to bury the dog beneath her hyacinths, or if Bob's childhood home was even still standing. She wondered if she could find her own childhood home if given a car and a full tank of gas and a perfect roadway lined with brilliant signs written specifically to direct her, and she decided no, she couldn't, and she felt herself drift lower underground, and a great fright crept over her.

SHIPWRECK

Peter wakes in the middle of the night again and hears the voices from old man's TV in the next apartment over, and as always the voices unnerve him for their similarity to those of two burglars beside his bedroom window plotting a sudden and violent break-in, or the residual echos of his ancestors, choruses of last words dissipating concentrically through space.

He sits up and checks his phone, which is dead, then touches his face, always burning with implacable anxiety. Finally, he gets up. The new routine is to fetch the tool box from the coat closet, camp out in the living room, and tinker on the hutch, a rundown family heirloom that, more than a century ago, had made the trip from Norway.

Sleep be damned. This old man, he's a terrible neighbor. Peter can't recall ever hearing noise from his previous neighbors, whom he had lived next to for almost a year, and even if he did, it was never as irritating as this, nor did it keep him in such a murky, gray somberness. The old man moved in two weeks ago with his dog, even though the building manager doesn't allow pets. What a hassle. Five days ago—a Saturday—Peter had disassembled the hutch in his living room board by board, set up two sawhorses outside, and stripped and sanded each piece on the apartment lawn. He stepped back to set a drawer face against the building and noticed a turd in the grass when he raised his shoe. It was white and covered in strange hair. Later in the day, he saw the old man at the mail boxes.

"I noticed you haven't been cleaning up after your dog," Peter said. "There aren't supposed to be any pets in the building."

"I was expecting a package today," the old man said. "I'm out of supplies," and he shuffled through the vestibule and disappeared around the corner. It was the first look Peter got at the man up close. His nose was awful, bulbous and red, veins blue and branched and throbbing as if the whole organ was about to burst.

Now, the hutch is strewn around the shadowy living room in pieces like broken floats of ice. It is an impressive piece of furniture: seven cabinets, ten drawers, nineteen brass pulls and ten brass escutcheons, acanthus leaves carved in the legs and fretwork. It had sat in his new living room for the better part of a year, hulking like a watchful Hun over the much humbler Ikea items. Somewhere along the way, he got the vague itch to rip it apart, give it a new look, and put it back together.

Through the wall, he hears the old man thumping around, picking things up and setting them down, some infernal clinking and frustrated stammering. The TV volume increases. Peter can't believe the old man is still up at this hour. Sometimes, he wonders about this man's family—where they went, if they are dead, if they ever even existed. Perhaps the old man still feels them there, a phantom presence fixed to his own like a limb that has been removed, or like a whisper in his ear, the faintest contrail of someone lost reverberating in memory. He puts away his tools after an hour of work, a bit more sleepy than when he started. The hutch isn't nearly finished and seems like maybe it never will be: two drawers is all he has put together. He wipes his brow on a sleeve and stands in the corner, eclipsed by shadow, listening for a moment to the old man's set through the wall. The muffled voices seep through.

He cannot make them out. He pictures the man watching infomercials, reclining in his only easy chair, preparing the telephone to purchase some stupid coin collection he can obsess over, or maybe to speak with a call-in psychic who will put him in communication with the dead. He supposes the old man is lonesome.

Through the kitchen window, while filling a glass of cold water to keep at bedside, Peter spots the old man with his dog, a fat lab gone gray in the muzzle. He stands away from the window, concealed by darkness, a molten core of heat warming the inside of his skull, and watches the man crouch down and put his hands on his knees, like a golfer inspecting the slope of a green. From this distance, the old man's nose seems more hideous than before, something growing from deep inside pushing its way through the surface of his skin. The dog squats, takes a shit. The man says something and scratches the dog behind its ears. They both shuffle back inside, the shit radiating like fissioned uranium in the glow of the orange streetlight.

Back in bed, Peter thinks lucidly of his uncle. It seems so recent—it was pretty recent, he guesses, ten or eleven years is all—that he peered around the corner into his grandmother's living room, where his mom sat before Hank handling rolls of gauze and tape, solemnly preparing a bandage for his face. They didn't speak. Sounds of tape tearing, one strip, then another. His mom worked deliberately, neatly fashioning the gauze bandage, her motions quick and practiced. Hank sitting dutifully as if preparing to set off on a long and lonesome voyage. He had turned toward Peter, and Peter had seen the cavity where Hank's nose used to be before the surgeon took it. This hole leaked oil that ignited in billowing orange blossoms. Sparks filled the room. From the carpet to the long mahogany beams in the ceiling: nothing but smoke and fire.

About a year ago, when he still lived back home, Peter's mother showed him his grandmother's photo albums. They sat together in the living room and shared a pot of coffee. The house belonged to his parents by then. They'd purchased it from his grandmother's estate for a competitive price and fixed it up nicely. It was quite a bit different from how it was when his grandmother and Hank, who was never fully competent, lived there together. The floors were hardwood now instead of the ugly orange shag. The brick fireplace was painted white. The mahogany beams were encased in oak veneer.

His mother picked a dogeared album from the stack and happened across a photograph of a sailing crew lined up on the deck of an early twentieth century Navy vessel. He couldn't make out all the faces. She told him the story of Irving, the ancestor who had died in a shipwreck off the Alaskan coast shortly after World War I, a decade before Peter's grandmother was born.

She turned the page, and there was another photo, this one of Irving handing another man a plank of wood as they fixed the carriage of a horse-drawn hearse, the year "1914" scratched in the corner. They wore hats and suspenders and white cotton shirts.

"Recognize him?" she said, running a finger across Irving's pointed nose and fleshy lips, his frosty eyes. "Uncanny, isn't it? Shave off the soup catcher and I would swear he's you."

It was true. Peter was a dead ringer for Irving. He pulled the photograph from its plastic sleeve and studied Irving's face. He'd heard the story many times before, and it had always fascinated him. Others, too, were fascinated by it. An iceberg concealed by dark waters, a hole torn through the ship's steel hull, thousands of gallons of whale blubber ignited on the ocean's breached surface. No survivors. The VFW in town was named for Irving. The story of his death had made him a hero to some.

"What else is in here?" Peter said. His mother flipped through the album. The pictures were more recent toward the back. Her as a little girl, pushing a bassinet full of kittens dressed in doll clothes. His grandmother in shadowy, smoky profile, reading receipts at her desk in the den. Hank, surrounded by relatives, blowing out candles on a birthday cake. Peter took out this photo, too, and turned it over. Someone—likely his grandmother—had written the details on the back: Hank's 30th birthday party, 1979. In the photo, Hank was dressed in a brown shirt with the top three buttons undone and white piping around the collar. His thick bottom lip was shiny with drool, and his mustache was slightly askew from clumsy trimming. He held a can of beer in his hand, a pack of Swisher Sweets in his breast pocket. The people around him were all smiling, elderly and liver-spotted, frozen in their applause.

The night after watching the man and his dog outside, Peter sets up a chair in front of the kitchen window. He narrows his eyes, gazing through the darkness—past the faucet and the miniature cacti decorating the window sill—laptop on his knees. His hands are sore from fitting boards and turning screws through unbroken planes of fresh lacquer. His face radiates heat. The property management company's website is opened on the browser, the blank form for residents to file complaints online. He fills in the slots requesting his name, building and unit, and telephone number while waiting. The cursor blinks in the white space in which residents are supposed to describe the details of their complaints.

He has a pretty good idea already what he will write: That this neighbor either does not know the rules of the apartment complex or does not care about them. That this man had intentionally dirtied the living premises of his neighbors and thus poses a distinct health risk to the immediate community. That this old man and his dog only seem to come out at night and haunt the parking lot, disturbing the things they touch, like ghosts.

Twenty minutes pass. No sign of the new neighbor. Usually Peter is asleep by now, or at least turning over in his sheets. He yawns once, then again with more force, then dozes, and when his head snaps upright—he is uncertain how much time has passed—the old man stands outside, leaning forward, stroking the long fur beneath the dog's neck. The man's faint kissing sounds filter through the window. The dog lumbers into the grass and squats. Its back arches, and it takes a couple of tiny steps before it stands and shakes itself and waddles toward its owner. The man extends his hand and gives the dog a treat. The two shuffle toward the door. They go inside.

"The hell you will," Peter says. He throws open the window. "Hey," he yells. "Hey you."

Either the old man does not hear, or he ignores him. The door latches without him so much as turning his head toward Peter's shouts.

"No," Peter says. "No."

He puts on sweatpants and running shoes and steps around the pieces of hutch, tripping slightly on a long board of the frame. One of the fluorescent bulbs in the hallway buzzes and flickers and emits an infected light that smears across the walls' pastel-green paint and the white wainscoting and door frames. He storms to the old man's door with a sickness in his gut, a white-hot prominence behind his face. If he opens his mouth, gamma rays might shoot out in hot, radioactive beams. He pounds three times, indifferent to the disturbance he might cause the other neighbors, none of whom ever give him trouble.

Behind the door: the movement of objects—plates or bowls being stacked, the smothered voice of a TV set turned up high. He wonders what kind of horrifying marks he'd see on his face in this light if forced to look in a mirror.

The old man comes to the door. He wears a white v-neck with an empty breast pocket, gray trousers belted halfway up his stomach, and a gold watch. His nose is ghastly up close. A leaking line of ruptures, red and yellow fluids mixing, pink like the color of exposed flesh. He smokes a cigarette.

"Yes?"

Peter looks past the neighbor's head, into the apartment. "I've noticed," he says, "that you haven't been picking up after your dog. There are rules, you know."

"Sam," the old man says, "is getting long at the tooth. Poor old Sam. Can't hardly see anymore."

"I'm prepared to file a complaint against you to the property managers."

"She was a pup when I got her." Peter feels him look up. Final Jeopardy is on the TV. Peter can't make out the question to the answer. The dog grunts and sighs from somewhere he can't see, then ambles over to them.

"Sam, come say hi."

"There aren't supposed to be any pets."

"There we go, Sammy. There we go. Say hi. There we go. Yes." The man digs a hand into his pocket and pulls out a bone-shaped biscuit for the dog.

Peter peers in further. There is a bookshelf on the other side of the TV, pictures of different children on each level. Long silver instruments on the coffee table, a fat glass bottle with hardly any neck set on its side, a tiny ship within it.

"Would you like a dish of ice cream?" the old man says.

"What's that?" Peter points to the stuff on the coffee table. Extreme heat. Looming spume of flame. He can swear his head is combusting from the inside out.

"Come in. Sit."

Peter looks down the hallway in each direction. Emptiness. He wipes his nose with the back of his hand.

"No. We have something we need to settle."

The neighbor grabs him by the arm. "You said you wanna talk. So come in. Let's talk."

Aside from the living room, the apartment is nearly empty: a couple boxes stacked against the lower cabinets in the kitchen; a greasy hot plate and a metal spatula on the counter top; a single plate slicked with gristle on the armrest of a small yellow easy chair. Peter sits on a metal folding chair beside the bookshelf. The old man seems to notice him surveying the things on the coffee table.

"A hobby," he says. "It makes the time pass." He lowers himself slowly into the easy chair, letting out a long sigh. The dog thumps down on a pillow on the floor, whacking its tail against the carpet. "I'm afraid it was destroyed during the move. I've been fiddling with putting it back together."

"That's too bad," Peter says. The man snuffs his cigarette in an ashtray beside the bottle and lights up another with a match. The flame twists and rights itself as he inhales. Peter holds his breath for a moment, lets it out, and breathes the toxic air. The stink reminds him of Hank's Swishers.

"Those will kill you, you know."

"They haven't yet." The old man reclines, letting out a wheezing laugh. "Have they, Sam?"

The complex is a no smoking community, too. Peter considers going back to his apartment to file his complaint. The pit of his stomach feels suddenly roving and bottomless, a great mysterious swirl. A darkness spins around his organs, pulling them into an ever widening inner depth. He leans forward, closer to the bottle, studying the tiny ship inside, half assembled.

"I've never seen one of these in person. How long does it take you?"

"The Umbria. She was lost in 1940. Captain scuttled her on purpose. It was a big suicide, more or less. Can you believe such a calamity?" The old man coughs. "Would you like to try?"

"Try?"

The old man turns down the TV. He says, "Start simple. Just a bit of the deck." He picks up the long silver forceps from the table, takes hold of a tiny wooden plank from the jewelry box beside the bottle, and applies a drop of glue to each end. "Place it there," he says. "Right on that spot. Right there where the deck ends. See? It's easy. I'll show you. Sam could do it." He slides the wooden board through the bottle's mouth, maneuvers it around the mast and sail, and places it atop the ship's tiny frame. "You try," he says. He picks up another piece of plank and hands the forceps to Peter. He says, "You saw. Just like I did it. It's so simple Sammy could do it."

Peter takes the instrument from the old man. It is difficult to see; the room's only light comes from the TV screen and the fixture in the kitchen. The jewelry box is monogrammed on the front: M.S.T., 6/17/2011 with Eternal Love, Happy 50th Anniversary. He studies the ship, the half-assembled deck and hull. He says, "It looks like something tore right through it."

"We're putting it together," the old man says. He points. "Right there. Just as I did."

The dog rises from its spot and circles, then plops back down. Peter slides the forceps into the bottle. His hand shakes. He finds the place on the frame where the old man wants him to situate the piece. His nose burns—he senses something, an abscess or a great sinkhole, spreading across his face, devouring the familiar contours into something monstrous and unrecognizable. Several other tools are laid out on the coffee table like a surgeon's silver tray.

He tries to concentrate on the ship. He extends the forceps deeper inside the bottle, finds the place where the little plank is supposed to go. He sets it down where he thinks it will rest properly, but it falls inside the ship's half-done hull when he lets go, toppling lengthwise, end over end.

"Shit," he says. He digs the forceps around the bottom of the bottle. The piece slips deeper inside. He says, "I lost it." He peers through the bottle's mouth. "I can't see it," he says. "Shit. Sorry."

The old man tells him it isn't any big deal. He gets up and fixes himself a dish of ice cream. He sits down and says not to worry about it. He says, "It's a tiny piece. I've got plenty." He spoons ice cream into his mouth. "Try again," he says. "I'll help you. It's okay. I'll help you do it."

He sets down his ice cream and takes the forceps from Peter. He prepares another plank, then, leaning forward, directs the tip to the bottle with his hands. "Slide it right through my fingers," he says. "I'll guide you."

Peter does as the old man tells him. He tweezes the the forceps through the old man's grip and sets the piece on the ship frame. It stays there as it is supposed to.

"There," the old man says. "You did it. Easy. Sam could do it. See?"

"Yes."

"You're fine. How did it feel? It felt fine?"

"It did," Peter says. He rubs his nose. His whole face might erupt into bright orange flame. He envisions what he might look like if the bones of his skull degrade and collapse inward, replaced with empty blackness. The old man's nose is horrible.

"Do another?" the old man says. He spoons a bite of ice cream and sets dish beside the bottle. "Do it yourself this time. See how it feels. I'll be here."

"I'll try it," Peter says. He prepares the forceps himself and breathes deeply. He gives the old man what he thinks will look like a sincere smile. He says, "It'll be fine."

POOL BOY

It's warm for September, seventy-five degrees at eleven in the morning. The pool boy is able to work without a shirt. The muck-vac hose sputters and jerks in his hands; the rich lady's kid likes to play with rubber torpedoes, and one of them is caught in the suction. This kid, Jackson, just started in the third grade. He suffers some condition, an extreme form of it, in which he screams made-up weather reports for different American cities. "Forty-five degrees in Topeka, rain in the afternoon, monsoon season tonight."

The rich lady strolls out of the house in her untied silk robe and striped bikini. The pool boy isn't sure how old she is. She seems like a young mother, but she is a widow. She had mentioned this to the pool boy once. Her husband was quite old and had died suddenly, and now the house feels empty, like an abandoned town.

Instead of oiling herself, or stretching out on one of the wicker chaises beside the shallow end, she lays down a towel, ties back her hair, and cranks out a hundred situps with perfect form. Elbows out. Shoulder blades back. Neck long. Synced breaths, inhaling when she lowers, exhaling when she sits up. Then she stands and struts toward the pool boy. She unties her hair and shakes it out. The sun hits her flat belly in just the right way, bouncing off the thin gauze of sweat like the reflections inside a kaleidoscope.

"You want a mimosa?" she says.

He stares into the pool, as if it is a giant eye.

"You got any Bud?" he says.

"It's early for that, isn't it?" She recedes inside through the long glass wall of windows and doors.

The pool boy's shift ends at five. The kid watches him load the company van with the muck-vac, the skimmer net, six leaf nets, and the telescoping pole. The happy song of an ice cream truck can be heard down the block. The kid has ice cream around his mouth. His outfit is a pinstriped baseball jersey with matching pinstriped shorts. He holds a sugar cone with strawberry running down his hand. His feet are bare and dirty. He asks the pool boy what he is doing, and if he can come. "Looks like a cold front is moving into the greater Albany-Schenectady area. Get the coats out of storage. It's going to be a chilly weekend."

It's a Friday. The pool boy drives the company van to his home and spends the evening eating fried catfish and Bud. His home is an efficiency apartment on the north side of the city. His downstairs neighbor screams each night. People on the street scream. The pool boy does not pony up for cable or internet access. He crosses his legs on the carpet, only passively attentive to the radio mewling weather reports in the kitchen. Instead, he thinks of noodling. Noodling is a special skill. Not everyone can do it as well as the pool boy. He learned it from his brother, who is dead. The two of them, they were a noodling team. Two young boys, ages nine and ten, noodling for catfish. To noodle properly, you use your body as the instrument of angling. There's no fancy equipment involved. You wade naked into the river and find a tangle of thickets or some salvage, like a partly submerged vehicle. No rod or reel or any high-tech gizmo like a depth finder or motorboat. Just you and the muddy current. You move about with your arms and feet on red-alert, feeling for a hole where the fish makes its home. When you find a fish at home, you dive in and wrestle with it and grab it by the body, or you stick your arm down its slimy throat until you are coated to the elbow in living fish. Then you pull the creature from its home. It will thrash. It won't want to leave its home. So you hold it tight to your body, like a long-lost brother. If you have a partner, he cheers you on. If not, you cherish the act yourself.

You take the fish someplace—the shore or your own home. You find your catfish cleaning gear, a used up cutting board crisscrossed with shallow slices, a six-inch barn spike hammered through it. The spike should face up. You hold the fish which you took from its home by the tail and raise it high above your head with both your quaking arms. Its slick back should be exposed, either to the sun or moon or the hanging garage lamp, depending on when and where you do this part. You drive it toward the board as if trying to hammer the spike back out, although the spike does not budge. It impales the fish through the skull and brain. The tip stares at you through the bottom of the fish's chin.

Despite being dead, the fish moves its lips in an O-shape that alternates between large and small, and it's possible you will think the fish is saying "Ow," over and over again, because its lips may strike you as being human, quite similar to your own, and being hammered headfirst onto a barn spike caked in fish brain is an awful thing.

The creature looks like it is suffering but is not, because it is dead. You lick your lips and run the skinny knife you use for such endeavors up the length of the fish's belly and use your free arm as an improvised retaining wall to keep the guts from spilling out, messy and red. You continue slicing and cutting until the skin is off and the meat is removed of all the small fish bones. You take a weekend to consume it with a case of Bud, twelve cans on Friday and twelve on Saturday, naked and alone in your home, ruminating on your happy past. And that's how you noodle. That's how the pool boy does it.

He fantasizes about noodling, dreams of it. Everyday

when he is at work. Every night as the Bud flows through him and his consciousness burns out. He thinks of the rich lady, too, passively. Her empty abdomen. Her bony shoulder blades which jut out like vestigial fins. The dark canal inside her that was the child's first home. A voice crawls from the kitchen forecasting sun.

He returns to work on Monday. There is a truck parked beside the pool and a team of Mexicans milling about the rich lady's plastic fronds. A man leans against the truck, observing the crew, writing things on a clipboard. The rich lady is out there, also. She holds a mimosa in one hand and directs the Mexicans to different parts of the yard with the other. Two of them uncoil the backwash hose and position its spout in the drain field behind the yard. One disappears behind the house, where the filtration system is kept. The last stays at poolside to make sure everything goes correctly. She barks orders. The sleeve of her robe slides up her slender arm. A single blue vein snakes from her elbow to her wrist.

The pool boy approaches the truck and sets down the muck-vac and the skimming net.

"What's all this?"

The truck rumbles and stinks of diesel exhaust. Some kind of pump is rigged in the bed. The man with the clipboard is fat. A cigarette hangs between his lips. His skin is ashen and pocked.

"Filling her in," the guy says. "The broad's idiot son fell in when he was sleepwalking. Almost drowned." He breathes smoke. "Fuck me, right?"

The pool boy imagines his arm elbow deep in the throat of an ice cream-covered boy. Slimy and sticky and pink, pulled from a submerged bank of strawberry, or Neapolitan.

"You," the rich lady says, pointing, "pool boy."

He picks up his gear and walks to her, sets it down, and leans against the brick edifice of the grill with his elbow bent. It is hot again. The voice on the radio said it would be hot for weeks to come.

"I apologize for this," she says. "I thought your company would let you know. I'm afraid I won't be needing your help anymore. Last night, Jackson," she says. She works her bottom lip. "Well, we narrowly avoided a terrible accident. I'll spare you the details. Anyway, I'm sure the gossip will get back to you." She finishes her drink and sets it on the grill, and the pool boy sees between the thin silk folds of her robe, her tan torso-skin taut and slick with the natural oils it has secreted, and he almost cries. "I'll pay you for the rest of the month," she says. "It's not fair that you should go unpaid."

"Works for me," he says.

"God, I can't handle this," she says. She rubs her face with both hands. "Come inside. I need to get my checkbook." He follows her through the glass wall and stands alone in the kitchen. Everything is white. The cabinets. The glossy floor. The appliances. The fridge has a TV screen built into its door. There is a blocky device on the countertop with touchscreen controls and a complicated row of silver handles. The table is white, too, decorated with a vase of white dahlias and a cloth runner the same cobalt blue as the pool liner.

He turns and notices the kid standing in the threshold to the living room. "Fog parting overnight," the kid says. "Should be smooth sailing from Macon to Atlanta for all you weekend travelers." This kid is short. His outfit today is a football uniform. A purple Culpepper jersey and tight white pants, purple socks, a toy helmet with viking horn decals on the sides. "Mostly cloudy and fifty-four degrees in Chicago this morning. Winds blowing from the northwest at fifteen miles per hour. Sunrise today was six fifty-eight a.m." The boy approaches him. He walks in a crooked line and runs his shoulder into the corner of the table. The vase of dahlias rattles and nearly tips. The pool boy isn't sure if the child is sleepwalking, or just strange. "You got any money?" the kid, Jackson, says. "I want an ice cream. Mom says she pays you well enough."

The pool boy crouches and meets his gaze. "You know who Daunte Culpepper is?"

"Unseasonably warm, even for Phoenix," Jackson says. "Yeah," he says. "He was quarterback."

"That's right," the pool boy says. "He was quarterback when I was your age."

"Fog parting overnight," he says. "Oh." He tilts the helmet back on his head and looks at the pool boy through the clunky gray face mask. "Unseasonably warm. So you got any money or what? Mom wonders what she pays you for."

The rich lady returns with a check for five hundred dollars. She gives it to the pool boy and apologizes again for the sudden dismissal. She goes outside and barks commands in Spanish.

How does a person adjust to a new routine? Who is he when his usual way of doing things is suddenly disrupted? What ought he do with himself?

The pool boy seeks something. Answers, maybe, or mystical insight.

"What's your favorite ice cream?" the pool boy says.

The child walks to the refrigerator, opens it, and peers in. He closes it without grabbing anything.

"Strawberry. It's always gotta be strawberry."

"My brother liked strawberry," the pool boy says. "He could eat a whole gallon and still want more." He thinks of fish whiskers on a boy-face, time-lapsed wrinkles, shadows increasing in the deepening skin-folds. "Come on," he says. "That ice cream truck is around here somewhere."

"Okay," the kid says. "Uncharacteristic hailstorms in Juneau. Let me get my shoes." He grabs the pool boy's hand and leads him through the living room, which is filled with glass tables and square furniture, to the foyer, just as white and fancy as the kitchen. More dahlias. A white bench. A crystal chandelier. The child digs around the floor of the coat closet, submerged from the waist up, as if searching for a fish home. The pool boy leans against the wall. After several moments, the child withdraws himself, holding a pair of toy football cleats. He slides them over his purple socks.

"You picked those right out," the pool boy says. "That was quick."

"They're my football shoes."

The child grabs his hand again and pulls him out the door, which they leave open. Happy music twinkles through the neighborhood. They stand at the end of the driveway, between brick stanchions of the rich lady's fence. The child hums along with the tune and smiles when the ice cream truck turns the corner. A swarm of kids come running. The truck stops several houses down. A jolly blue walrus has been painted on its side.

"Give me a five," the child says. The pool boy fishes around in his pocket, pulls out two one-dollar bills, and hands them to him. The child takes off running with a neighbor girl who comes whipping around a square hedgerow, dressed as a ballerina. The pool boy watches them crowd the truck. A man dressed as an old-fashioned soda jerk laughs with them and plunges his hand into a freezer, concealed by the truck itself. The jerk dispenses varieties of ice cream: orange-flavored push-pops, root beer Popsicles, hot fudge sundaes topped with whipped cream and cherries. Jackson returns with a paper cup of scooped strawberry.

"You didn't give me enough for a cone," the kid says. "Whopper of a squall in Dayton. I couldn't get a cone." He spoons strawberry into his mouth. They stroll across the green lawn together. The child goes inside and locks the door behind him.

Even though it is a Monday, the pool boy stops at the liquor store. He finished all twenty-four cans of Bud between

Friday and Saturday, and he needs Bud. He needs catfish. The Monday girl clerk is different from the Friday girl clerk.

"Where's the Friday girl at?" he says, holding out a twenty.

"Who?" She rings him up and spits her gum on the floor.

The case of beer sits in the passenger seat, secured with the seat belt, its cardboard handle torn and bent. He drinks six Buds while he drives around the suburban backstreets, gawking at the homes. The homes light up one by one. After a while, he travels into the city, across one bridge, then another. The skyline glows, gold and blue against the black sky. He parks the company van in a low dark clearing on the university campus, beneath the bridge students jump from when they're homesick or fail a test. The skyscrapers are eclipsed by a shadowed cliff on the far bank of the river. He strips naked and drinks another Bud and wades into the water. The surface ripples and fractures the long orange reflections of the streetlights above. His penis and scrotum shrivel. His nipples pucker and become hard as ball bearings. He massages his forearms under the black surface. He imagines his hand is Jackson's hand, that, if he could see it, it would appear small and misshapen, extraterrestrial. His toes sink into the mud. He imagines his hand is tan and slender, the rich lady's. He strokes his forearm as if it belongs to someone else and sinks his knees into the river bottom. This is what his arm would feel like, he thinks, if another person touched it. The current pushes against him. He discovers a tangle of poplar branches and searches for a fish home. His feet feel sticks and weeds, soot and mud and large rocks. His hands feel in greater detail. Hard. Slimy. Lifeless. After several minutes, his foot gets caught by a wide hole, a fish home. He whimpers and dives underwater, thrusts his arm into the hole, and withdraws a fistful of clay. The fish isn't home. Maybe it is submerged deeper in the mud, hiding with its brothers. A whole slick clan of fish-brothers, burrowed in earth. He drifts in circles and lets his limbs go slack like a clump of weeds.

He clambers up the bank. Water rolls off his body and splashes loudly into itself. He is hungry. He leans against the company van and drinks another Bud. Sometimes, he wonders if a part of him had been left behind when he was born, something lodged in the skin-pink walls of an unknowable uterus, crushed by that impassable skin fortress, something that would help him understand. He looks at the river and, with one hand, studies the contours of the empty other.

The next day, he parks the company van half a block down, so the rich lady cannot detect him. He had woken up with the thought in his head, "I am a worm. I am something people see and then they shriek."

The backyard is full of yellow-vested men operating heavy machinery. There is a lot of shouting and hissing engines. Crashes. Plumes of dust. One of the machines is a giant arm on moving treads. At the end of the arm a large steel spike vibrates and shatters the concrete pool wherever it touches. The demolition sounds like a machine gun. A man follows behind on an excavator, scooping the broken slabs and moving them to a pile beside the rich lady's plastic fronds.

The pool boy slinks through the glass wall. The sun is hot and white. He stands in the kitchen, in assembled whiteness. The boy, Jackson, sits at the white table reading comics on a touchscreen tablet. He is dressed in a one-piece pajama set, a Ninja Turtle. His feet dangle, covered in green fabric.

"Nothing but sun in Reno," he says. "You're the one who stares at Mom. Smog advisory."

"You want an ice cream?"

"She's upstairs." The child does not look up. His small fingers tap the screen, tap the screen.

"I got some money for an ice cream. Your mama paid

me to look after you this afternoon."

"The entire bay area remains threatened with landslides," the boy says. "Okay," he says. "It better be strawberry."

The child leads him into the foyer. The pool boy watches him slide a pair of tiny leather yacht shoes over the feet of his pajamas.

"Aren't you going to change clothes?" the pool boy says.

"No," he says. "You can't make me."

The pool boy drives them around the neighborhood. Ow, he thinks. He thinks, cut me up and seal me in a can, but leave my lips to speak. He thinks, a can with a nice label, one that will appeal to young mothers.

They can not find the happy song of the ice cream truck.

"Oh well," the pool boy says.

"The upper plains will see smoke on the horizon from fires in the west," the kid says. He grips the armrests and presses his head against the dashboard. "I want an ice cream. I want an ice cream. I want an ice cream." He kicks off his yacht shoes.

"Buckle your seat belt," the pool boy says. He thinks of pink rubber gloves. Tubes. A cement desert stippled with plastic fronds. "What would you do if you had a brother of your own?" he says. "One that was the same age as you?"

"I want an ice cream. Mom prefers the Mexicans to you."

The pool boy recalls a cabin. He isn't sure where it was, or who it belonged to. There were stuffed fish and boat oars mounted on the walls. Empty beer cans lined the kitchen counter. He and his brother had walked the shoreline, hitting dead fish with sticks.

"I bet you miss your dad," he says. "Something awful must have happened. I know how it is."

"I want an ice cream. Hail the size of soccer balls."

The pool boy pulls onto the interstate. The kid whines about ice cream and issues false weather reports. The pool boy explains noodling.

"It connects you to nature and the parts yourself you don't really know about. You ever been noodling before?"

"Nope."

"You gotta be careful not to let the river suck you under. You gotta be careful the fish doesn't wrestle with you and fill your lungs up. A little boy like you, it's a terrible thing."

The pool boy needs a Bud. He needs a Bud to quench his thirst. He thinks of his brother, the way the hair lay on the surface, bobbing in the slow ripples, and his mouth goes dry, just like it did back then, when he could not summon words, neither to cry or yell, standing on the shore instead, O-mouthed, dumb. Drown me in suds, he thinks. Weigh me down and leave me at the bottom.

"You got a nice mom," the pool boy says. "She told me that you're lonesome and it causes you to act funny. I get it. I know how it goes."

The kid wilts, as if he is a slug and the pool boy has dumped salt on him.

The pool boy exits near a shopping mall, noses along a frontage road, and parks at the Walmart.

"Lightning in Dallas. Mom says this is where Somalians shop."

"We can shop here, too. It's fine to shop here. I shop here, sometimes. We need to get you set up, is all. For noodling. Put your shoes on. It ain't so bad."

They load a cart with sugar cones and strawberry ice cream, then wind their way to the sporting goods department at the back of the store. Little turtle man, the pool boy thinks. Little green sidekick. They stop at a shelf packed with fishing poles and synthetic bait. Glittery purple grub worms with hooks in their torsos. Hardened drops of plastic painted to look like minnows. Red and white trolling spoons embossed with the face of a cartoon Satan.

"We don't need this stuff," the pool boy says. "We don't need no fancy gear. Me and you, we use our hands."

The kid ignores him, peeling open the ice cream container and immersing his hand in the strawberry instead. He pulls up a wad, thick like clay, and sticks it in his mouth. His lips smack as he chews, pink strings of spit stretching from the roof of his mouth to his mandible. He winces and pitches forward.

"Ow," he says. "Rain showers. Ow. My head."

"Slow down," the pool boy says. "We got plenty of time."

He pulls a set of Neoprene waders off the top shelf.

"These should fit," the pool boy says. He holds them up against the boy's lean frame. "I don't use them, myself, but you might wanna stay covered."

"Whatever," the boy says. "Bad news, Boston. Extreme cold is expected for the rest of the week." He eats another knot of strawberry and cringes in pain. The pool boy tosses the waders into the cart, pays, and loads the van with their supplies. Snacks stacked on a crate of skimmer baskets. Waders slung over the muck-vac.

"You ready?" the pool boy says. "I like having a partner again. It's a nice change."

The child holds the ice cream in his lap. He scoops it with his hands and wipes them on the seat.

"Ow," he says. "Ow. The barometric pressure is variable for the Boise metro area. Ow. Higher in the north, going down as you head south. Ow. I forgot my phone."

The van glides along the frontage road. He stops at a liquor store, different from the usual one. He purchases a case of Bud, opens it in the parking lot, and pulls out two, still chilled. He slides the box on its side beneath the child's feet.

"For you to rest on," he says. "Careful they don't spill."

He puts the van in gear. They continue across several bridges.

It seems like something could swallow them whole. The pool boy doesn't know what. The van could be like a floating swan-boat. It could pass through a set of disembodied lips, looming pink and vertically, into a black tunnel. The lips could speak.

"Ow," they could say. "Ow. Damn you for going through." Inside, the swan floats past a diorama of primping fashion models arranged among plastic fronds, lit red from beneath. They gather at the sight of the boat and crank out situps in their string bikinis. A carnal drum beat originates from inside the pool boy's white gut. It is steady and grows. It consumes him from the neck down. He is guided by the turtle child, who speaks, "These are the things you see. What else is there to know?"

Downtown is black and glossy against the gray sky. The light wanes. Smears of orange and purple in the fissures between skyscrapers. The pool boy drowns his throat in Bud. Amber waves crash down into his core.

"Yum," he says. He looks at the boy, slumped against the window. "One day, when you're old enough, I'll let you try."

"Ow," the boy says. "My stomach hurts." He eats another pink fistful. "Ow. Duluth can expect showery weather late Thursday night through Friday evening. It's gonna be wet. Ow."

The ice cream tub gapes empty on his lap.

"Look at you," the pool boy says. "You finished it." He gulps the remainder of Bud. "Maybe you can let me in on it next time?"

The van creeps through the campus side streets.

"Ow," the boy says. "My stomach hurts. I need Mama."

The pool boy parks in the clearing beneath the bridge. He thinks of cradled arms, hairless.

"Here we are," he says. He opens the second Bud. He drinks it in three swigs.

"I need Mama. Ow."

"Quit joking around," the pool boy says. He opens

the back door, gathers the waders in his arms, and brings them to the child. "Here," he says. "Put these on. They'll do wonders."

"Dust storms in Fresno. Ow." The child throws the ice cream tub to the grass. He steps down and holds his belly. The pool boy puts a hand on his shoulder. The child keels forward and vomits on the fender.

"Woosh," the pool boy says. "Look out below." He goes for the Bud and has another.

"Ow," the child says. "That's better. Mist this evening in Portland. That's Portland, Oregon, folks, not Portland, Maine. When are we going home?"

"I wanna try something." The pool boy belches. He laughs. He holds out the waders. "Put these on."

"Over my turtle jammies?"

"That's right," the pool boy says. He remembers a fish that wouldn't die. His brother bludgeoned its head but it wouldn't die.

"I need Mama. When are we going home?" The child describes hailstorms, green squalls ripping through central Oklahoma.

"Afterwards." The pool boy crushes the empty Bud can with the heel of his boot. He grinds it into the dirt. "I wanna try something."

The child, Jackson, slides off his yacht shoes and slowly inserts his legs into the waders, the left, then right. They fit his body tightly. He grins.

"I got a new shell," he says. "A shell over my shell. Watch out, Toledo. A storm front is heading your way. One as thick and dangerous as my mother's peach cobbler."

The pool boy chuckles. He feels a concavity growing within him. A flesh purse for all the things inside himself he can neither see nor understand. The child's vomit sprawls across the dirt and grass like an obliterated fish brain.

"Come closer," the pool boy says. He squats. He reaches

for the child. They touch arms across that little, startlingly muscled body. He clasps his hands around the boy's midriff and caresses the grooves of his own knuckles, skin and bone filled with skin and bone. The bridge lights turn on. Their orange reflections dance with the river's current. They twinkle and elongate.

"Here we go," the pool boy says. "Here we go." He stands and lumbers to the water, instructing the child to use his arms, to feel for gaps in the muddy, submerged bank.

"You feel for a set of lips," he says, "or a slimy whisker. That's how you know they're home."

They wade in: a single creature, a two-bodied monster fused at the belly by the moving water, or by the moment itself. A flesh entanglement. One borne from the other, because it has always existed inside the other. The pool boy sinks lower. His knees touch bottom, then his thighs, knocked against by the boy's slight heels.

"Feel," he says. "Feel around some."

The boy shivers. He speaks:

"Meteor shower over Dallas-Fort Worth. Fog parting in Denver. Whipping squall. Whipping squall."

The two of them go under, into the river's darkness. The surface ripples. The reflections glisten on the waves.

ACKNOWLEDGEMENTS

There are a number of people without whom this book would never have seen the light of day. Ashton Allen and Kim Verhines of SFA Press saw something in the slush pile worth pursuing. I am greatly indebted to them for taking a chance on this book. Roger Sheffer gave me indispensable advice while I was working on the stories included and those left out. If there is a better line editor than Roger, I have yet to meet them. Geoff Herbach encouraged me to follow my instincts. Stan Rivkin pushed me further than I knew I could go. Jon McConnell has been an advocate I did not expect to have. Of course, implicit in all of these "thank yous" is my gratidude to Connie, who sparked my interest in this whole endeavor.

I would also like to thank the Sundress Academy for the Arts for their support of this project, as well as the editors of the magazines in which some of these stories originally appeared: *Split Lip Magazine* ("Call Me Randy," "Physically Alarming Men"), *J Journal* ("Golden Years"), *Corium Magazine* ("Things that Drop"), *Four Way Review* ("Rainy River"), *Western Humanities Review* ("Empire"), *3:AM Magazine* ("Doctor on a Hill"), *Belmont Story Review* ("Cadillac Man"), and *The Pinch* ("Pool Boy").

Finally, thank you to my family. None of this would have been possible without you. I owe my greatest debt to Melanie. You support me for reasons I cannot begin to understand.